Florida Stories

Tales from the Tropics

Florida Stories

Tales from the Tropics

Edited by JOHN *and* KIRSTEN MILLER

CHRONICLE BOOKS

SAN FRANCISCO

Printed in the United States of America.
Page 178 constitutes a continuation of the copyright page.

Library of Congress Cataloging-in-Publication Data
Florida stories: tales from the tropics / edited by John and Kirsten Miller
p. cm.
ISBN 0-8118-0457-7 (pbk.)
1. Florida—Literary collections. 2. American literature—Florida.
I. Miller, John, 1959- . II. Miller, Kirsten.
PS558. F6F66 1993
813.008' 032759—dc20

93-327
CIP

Editing and design: Big Fish Books
Composition: Jennifer Petersen, Big Fish Books

Distributed in Canada by Raincoast Books,
112 East Third Avenue, Vancouver, B.C. V5T 1C8

10 9 8 7 6 5 4 3 2 1

CHRONICLE BOOKS
275 FIFTH STREET
SAN FRANCISCO, CA 94103

CONTENTS

Special thanks to Bob Shacochis and Max at El Loro Verde Lounge, Key West

Bob Shacochis

PARADISE. ANYBODY FOUND it yet? Anybody got a clue?
Well, yes and no.

It is an innately mischievous question, this one we ask each
other about heaven on earth. If you asked me where it was, I
wouldn't answer Florida, though someone from Ohio just might.
Perhaps it's accurate to say, however, that any serious quest for a para-
disiacal destination begins—and more often ends, by default—here
in the Sunshine State, where northern proprieties are unbuttoned by
what Isaac Bashevis Singer has described as our "planned hedonism,"
whimsically pursued within a master plan of some very heady bio-
spheric seductions.

There's our weather, for instance; sublime and, alternately,

---

*Bob Shacochis went tropical early on: all of this Virginian's books are set
in Florida and the tropics. Shacochis won the American Book Award in
1985 for his novel* Easy in the Islands.

when the Big Wind blows, sublimely wicked—it giveth and it taketh away. It would not be out of order to erect a billboard at the Georgia-Florida state line, advising southbound travelers: *Begin Removing Clothes and Inhibitions Now.* Off come the sweaters at Jacksonville, off come the shoes and socks at Daytona, off comes almost everything at Fort Lauderdale, and by the time you've descended to Key West, you've shucked so many layers of yourself that off come decency, common sense, and whatever civilized behavior you once adhered to. Some travelers would say it's not a bad trade.

There's our landscape too, primordial and lascivious. The pine and oak forests of the north, cloaked in the ghostly enchantment of Spanish moss and color-splattered with camellias. For the 16th century explorer Cabeza de Vaca, here was a country "remote and malign," watered by crystal clear lakes, roamed by wild beasts and hostile Indians. It's where I live today, and I can tell you that timeless sense of wilderness remains largely intact—the Johnny Weismuller Tarzan movies were filmed just a few miles down the road, at Wakulla Springs, where nothing much has changed in millennia.

There's the sensual flora of the south, the plant world's pornography, bending under the fleshy weight of phallic fruits and labial blossoms, oozing exotic perfumes. "Those secretive palms in their pink skies" that framed Elizabeth Bishop's field of vision. There are the Everglades' mangrove swamps and vast watery savannahs, where you might reasonably expect to see *Australopithecus* loping toward the refuge of a cypress hammock.

And don't forget the beaches, our dazzling sugar-white sun-crazed beaches, looped around the state like a lace collar at the throat of a temptress whose dangerous, spellbinding beauty, like Joan Didion's Miami, fades and reemerges with the movement of the water and the clouds and the sun.

There is, finally, here in Florida, what Wallace Stevens calls "the genius of the sea," and that genius nourishes the most reckless, free, and noble parts of who we Floridians are. The sea is also responsible for our state being a place where people and things wash up— shipwrecks, Audubon's pirates, bales of marijuana, John Sayles's Cuban exiles, Haitians, tourists, retirees, somebody else's revolution, conquistadores, mermaids, fugitives, crazies, criminals and, of course, writers.

Narcotics are part of the modern vernacular down here, yet inspiration has always seemed to be the official state drug, stirred directly into the orange juice for mass consumption. For Hawthorne, Florida was an original source of magical realism, its jungles populated with fables and fabulous enterprise, and for Didion, a place like Miami "seemed not a city at all but a tale, a romance of the tropics, a kind of waking dream in which any possibility could and would be accommodated."

It's true, I think, that Florida's where many refugees from the daily grind come looking for a place to soothe the deep yearning in their hearts, a place that fulfills the dream of sanctuary, a place that heals their unseen wounds. Perhaps it's that ethos of accommodation that makes Florida a frontier for our fantasies, drawing us deeper into the lives we want for ourselves, and consequently makes the state a hothouse of stories and adventures, told and retold, about nature and blood and money and power and love. No raconteur can make us too colorful, too ingenious, too ambitious, too deluded, too bizarre or brutal, too mixed up and mixed together, or too corrupt. We farm snakes and alligators, parrots and orchids. We tell a lot of lies about fish, and about fountains of eternal youth. There's a lot of local news in the papers down here about narcotraffickers, about dictators and guerillas and the political intrigues so feverishly essential to the texture of the tropics. Our neighbors run dope or guns or they run a front company for the CIA or God. They dress in *guayaberas* or thong bikinis or camouflage. They never take off their sunglasses, or their edge.

We're overrun with the most dire, extreme, virtuous, gorgeous, volatile, marvelous and squirrelly characters, down here at the bottom of the nation, and when you get fed up with them all, or punch drunk, or intractably hooked by the dream, you get on a boat and go, like Hemingway, farther south into the myth, down to the Tortugas, across the Stream to the Grand Bahama Banks, to Cuba, to the Turks and Caicos, to the Windward Passage, no farther than the fingertips of your imagination, blown by the tradewinds to a place where the sun is always overhead, to a place you've not yet been able to imagine—the throne of pleasure or the heart of darkness.

Has the global village become too familiar for such illusions? Florida says, Don't bet on it.

And yet Florida's what we settle for, a mostly sane compromise, when we run out of options, fail in our quest . . . or when we're foolish enough to succeed, only to discover that paradise is just another place to leave. Because the angels are as sinful as you are, and don't want you there anyway. Because there are no cheeseburgers. Because paradise is actually the end of the imagination, and Florida definitely is not. Rather, it's border territory, a land poised on the brink of the unknown and washed by the tides of desire, and at the close of those lives we dared imagine for ourselves, the Florida we settle into is an existential state of reminiscence, peopled by folks like Joy Williams's Gurdjieff who retire into endless nostalgia, occasionally commanding themselves, *Try to enjoy Florida*, and any working defini-tion of paradise lost must incorporate a place that encourages us to recall, in generous detail, what it is we've left behind. That's the place where Florida exists, on the threshold of that spirit, and its door opens upon the deep blue currents of memory, and the warmest lati-tudes of anticipation.

John James Audubon

IN THE CALM of a fine moonlight night, as I was admiring the beauty of the clear heavens, and the broad glare of light that glanced from the trembling surface of the waters around, the officer on watch came up and entered into conversation with me. He had been a turtler in other years, and a great hunter to boot, and although of humble birth and pretensions, energy and talent, aided by education, had raised him to a higher station. Such a man could not fail to be an agreeable companion, and we talked on various subjects, principally, you may be sure, birds and other natural productions. He told me he once had a disagreeable adventure, when looking out for game, in a certain cove on the shores of the Gulf of Mexico; and, on my

---

Writer and naturalist John James Audubon traveled to Florida in the 1830s in search of material for his drawings. But he stumbled on something quite different: this story, excerpted from his Ornithological Biography, *was told to him late one night in the Keys by a grizzled sailor on watch.*

expressing a desire to hear it, he willingly related to me the following particulars, which I give you, not perhaps precisely in his own words, but as nearly so as I can remember.

"Towards evening, one quiet summer day, I chanced to be paddling along a sandy shore, which I thought well fitted for my repose, being covered with tall grass, and as the sun was not many degrees above the horizon, I felt anxious to pitch my mosquito bar or net, and spend the night in this wilderness. The bellowing notes of thousands of bull-frogs in a neighbouring swamp might lull me to rest, and I looked upon the flocks of blackbirds that were assembling as sure companions in this secluded retreat.

I proceeded up a little stream, to insure the safety of my canoe from any sudden storm, when, as I gladly advanced, a beautiful yawl came unexpectedly in view. Surprised at such a sight in a part of the country then scarcely known, I felt a sudden check in the circulation of my blood. My paddle dropped from my hands, and fearfully indeed, as I picked it up, did I look towards the unknown boat. On reaching it, I saw its sides marked with stains of blood, and looking with anxiety over the gunwale, I perceived to my horror, two human bodies covered with gore. Pirates or hostile Indians I was persuaded had perpetrated the foul deed, and my alarm naturally increased; my heart fluttered, stopped, and heaved with unusual tremors, and I looked towards the setting sun in consternation and despair. How long my reveries lasted I cannot tell; I can only recollect that I was roused from them by the distant groans of one apparently in mortal agony. I felt as if refreshed by the cold perspiration that oozed from every pore, and I reflected that though alone, I was well armed, and might hope for the protection of the Almighty.

Humanity whispered to me that, if not surprised and disabled, I might render assistance to some sufferer, or even be the means of saving a useful life. Buoyed up by this thought, I urged my canoe on shore, and seizing it by the bow, pulled it at one spring high among the grass.

The groans of the unfortunate person fell heavy on my ear, as I cocked and reprimed my gun, and I felt determined to shoot the first that should rise from the grass. As I cautiously proceeded, a hand was raised over the weeds, and waved in the air in the most supplicating manner. I levelled my gun about a foot below it, when the next moment, the head and breast of a man covered with blood were convulsively raised, and a faint hoarse voice asked me for mercy and help! A death-like silence followed his fall to the ground. I surveyed every object around with eyes intent, and ears impressible by the slightest sound, for my situation that moment I thought as critical as any I had ever been in. The croaking of the frogs, and the last blackbirds alighting on their roosts, were the only sounds or sights; and I now proceeded towards the object of my mingled alarm and commiseration.

Alas! the poor being who lay prostrate at my feet, was so weakened by loss of blood, that I had nothing to fear from him. My first impulse was to run back to the water, and having done so, I returned with my cap filled to the brim. I felt at his heart, washed his face and breast, and rubbed his temples with the contents of a phial, which I kept about me as an antidote for the bites of snakes. His features, seamed by the ravages of time, looked frightful and disgusting; but he had been a powerful man, as the breadth of his chest plainly shewed. He groaned in the most appalling manner, as his breath struggled through the mass of blood that seemed to fill his throat. His dress plainly disclosed his occupation:—a large pistol he had thrust into his bosom, a naked cutlass lay near him on the ground, a red silk handkerchief was bound over his projecting brows, and over a pair of loose trousers he wore fisherman's boots. He was, in short, a Pirate.

My exertions were not in vain, for as I continued to bathe his temples, he revived, his pulse resumed some strength, and I began to hope that he might perhaps survive the deep wounds he had received. Darkness, deep darkness, now enveloped us. I spoke of making a fire. "Oh!, for mercy's sake," he exclaimed, "don't." Knowing, however, that under existing circumstances, it was expedient for me to do so, I left him, went to his boat, and brought the rudder, the benches, and the oars, which with my hatchet I soon splintered. I then struck a light, and presently stood in the glare of a blazing fire. The Pirate seemed struggling between terror and gratitude for my assistance; he desired me several times in half English and Spanish to put out the flames, but after I had given him a draught of strong spirits, he at length became more composed. I tried to staunch the blood that flowed from the deep gashes in his shoulders and side. I expressed my regret that I had no food about me, but when I spoke of eating he sullenly waved his head.

My situation was one of the most extraordinary that I have ever been placed in. I naturally turned my talk towards religious subjects, but, alas, the dying man hardly believed in the existence of God. "Friend," said he, "for friend you seem to be, I have never studied the ways of Him of whom you talk. I am an outlaw, perhaps you will say a wretch—I have been for many years a Pirate. The instructions of my parents were of no avail to me, for I have always believed that I was born to be a most cruel man. I now lie here, about to die in the weeds, because I long ago refused to listen to their many admonitions. Do not shudder when I tell you—these now useless hands murdered the mother whom they had embraced. I feel that I have deserved the pangs of the wretched death that hovers over me; and I am thankful that one of my kind will alone witness my last gaspings."

A fond but feeble hope that I might save his life, and perhaps assist in procuring his pardon, induced me to speak to him on the subject. "It is all in vain, friend—I have no objection to die—I am glad that the villains who wounded me were not my conquerors—I want no pardon from *any one*—Give me some water, and let me die alone."

With the hope that I might learn from his conversation something that might lead to the capture of his guilty associates, I returned from the creek with another capful of water, nearly the whole of which I managed to introduce into his parched mouth, and begged him, for the sake of his future peace, to disclose his history to me. "It is impossible," said he, "there will not be time; the beatings of my heart tell me so. Long before day, these sinewy limbs will be motion-less. Nay, there will hardly be a drop of blood in my body; and that blood will only serve to make the grass grow. My wounds are mortal, and I must and will die without what you call confession."

The moon rose in the east. The majesty of her placid beauty impressed me with reverence. I pointed towards her, and asked the Pirate if he could not recognise God's features there. "Friend, I see what you are driving at," was his answer,—"you, like the rest of our enemies, feel the desire of murdering us all.—Well—be it so—to die is after all nothing more than a jest; and were it not for the pain, no one, in my opinion, need care a jot about it. But, as you really have befriended me, I will tell you all that is proper."

Hoping his mind might take a useful turn, I again bathed his temples and washed his lips with spirits. His sunk eyes seemed to dart fire at mine—a heavy and deep sigh swelled his chest and struggled through his blood-choked throat, and he asked me to raise him for a little. I did so, when he addressed me somewhat as follows, for, as I have told you, his speech was a mixture of Spanish, French and English, forming a jargon, the like of which I had never heard before, and which I am utterly unable to imitate. However I shall give you the substance of his declaration.

"First tell me, how many bodies you found in the boat, and what sort of dresses they had on." I mentioned their number, and described their apparel. "That's right," said he, "they are the bodies of the scoundrels who followed me in that infernal Yankee barge. Both rascals they were, for when they found the water too shallow for their craft, they took to it and waded after me. All my companions had been shot, and to lighten my own boat I flung them overboard, but as I lost time in this, the two ruffians caught hold of my gun wale, and struck on my head and body in such a manner, that after I had disabled and killed them both in the boat, I was scarce able to move. The other villains carried off our schooner and one of our boats, and perhaps ere now have hung all my companions whom they did not kill at the time. I have commanded my beautiful vessel many years, captured many ships, and sent many rascals to the devil. I always hated the Yankees, and only regret that I have not killed more of them.—I sailed from Matanzas.—I have often been in concert with others. I have money without counting, but it is buried where it will never be found, and it would be useless to tell you of it." His throat filled with blood, his voice failed, the cold hand of death was laid on his brow, feebly and hurriedly he muttered, "I am a dying man, farewell."

Alas! It is painful to see death in any shape; in this it was horrible, for there was no hope. The rattling of his throat announced the moment of dissolution, and already did the body fall on my arms with a weight that was insupportable. I laid him on the ground. A mass of dark blood poured from his mouth; then came a frightful groan, the last breathing of that foul spirit; and what now lay at my feet in the wild desert?—a mangled mass of clay!

The remainder of that night was passed in no enviable mood; but my feelings cannot be described. At dawn I dug a hole with the paddle of my canoe, rolled the body into it, and covered it. On reaching the boat I found several buzzards feeding on the bodies, which I in vain attempted to drag to the shore. I therefore covered them with mud and weeds, and launching my canoe, paddled from the cove with a secret joy for my escape, overshadowed with the gloom of mingled dread and abhorrence."

Joy Williams

GURDJIEFF IN THE SUNSHINE STATE

THIS IS ENDLESS, G. thinks. He is sitting at a table in the lounge area of a roller-skating rink in Florida, watching the children skate. On the table are french fries, cheese-filled pretzel logs, two chicken enchiladas and a glass of water with no ice. *How strange that I am in this place*, G. thinks. He wishes, in a way, that he were back in Atlantis, but there are so many Germans there! With those panting, slobbering dogs all trained to sniff out pharmaceuticals! *Try to enjoy Florida*, he commands himself. Outside there are oranges and pelicans and snake farms. And sharks' teeth! Impossible to walk along the beaches of Florida without picking up sharks' teeth between one's toes. Inside, he is very comfortable in the air conditioning. He wears a

---

Joy Williams is the author of Escapes, *a book of short stories, and three novels, including* States of Grace, *which was nominated for the 1974 National Book Award. She lives part-time in Florida and masterminded the definitive* The Florida Keys: A History and Guide.

heavy overcoat with a tightly curled lamb's-wool collar and a Cossack cap. In his pocket are forty-seven rolls of film. *I've got to get these things developed*, G. thinks. There comes a point . . .

THERE ARE A hundred preadolescents with clear blue eyes and cute knees tearing around the rink at great speed. The preadolescents make G. feel tired. *Questions, questions, questions,* G. thinks. It's a blessing answers are not required. G. strokes his large mustache. *A baked potato is more intelligent than a raw potato,* he muses. *I think.*

G. FEELS A little vague. He's been thinking about the Hindus too much. He would like to go to India again but believing in the Eternal Now as he must, he's afraid of the Thugs. The British stamped out Thuggee in 1840 but that doesn't help G. The Thugs strangled travelers with scarves and threw them down wells. They did not kill everybody. There were certain restrictions. They did not strangle women or lepers or the blind or the mutilated or anyone driving a cow or stonecutters or shoemakers. G. counts these types on his fingers. He is none of these people. He shudders. *Better stay away from India*, he thinks. G. is afraid of Thugs. He also fears mud. The dreams he has about mud he wouldn't tell a living soul. *Better squash this kind of thinking*, G. decides.

G. WAS USED to having dead people around him. He was used to admirers saying, "All the people around you seem dead." He got used to that kind of praise. No one says anything like that to him here. No one seems to notice him.

THE MUSIC IS deafening. Sometimes a song is played that is a little slower but no less loud than the others and the preadolescents dance to it on their roller skates. G. loves dancing. He taps his foot and strokes his mustache. The dark waters of the Tab imprisoned in the paper cup jiggle on the tabletop. *I'm in Florida!* he thinks. He loves Florida, the cold center of it. *Dance the orange,* he says enthusiastically. *Uh-oh,* he thinks. *That belongs to someone else. That German poet. Those Germans are everywhere,* he thinks with irritation. In Mexico, they were in the pyramids, in the swimming pools, in the markets buying tin lamps. In Paris, they were in the Louvre, applying Freudian theory to da Vinci, standing in front of "The Holy Family," yelling, "I see the vulture, do you see the vulture!" They were even on the Riviera, eating trout. G. has to admit, however, that they make wonderful cars. *Those BMWs,* he thinks, with a thrill of pleasure. He wishes he could dump his stupid car somewhere and get a Jaguar. *Dance the orange,* he recalls with embarrassment. He blushes but no one can tell.

KATHERINE MANSFIELD COMES up to the table and sits down, gloomy as ever. He does not offer her a cigarette. She may be asleep but one never knows. No need to insult her. He smiles. *Isn't it great to be young,* he says, indicating the skaters, just making chitchat. Katherine Mansfield looks at him with consternation. *When will she cheer up!* G. sighs. He bends forward. *Impossibility is sign of truth,* he hisses. *That which can be expressed cannot be true. How many times I have to tell you that!* "I was a writer," Katherine Mansfield says with dignity. She goes away.

G. LONGS FOR a glass of Calvados from one of those twenty-seven bottles he found covered over with a mixture of lime, sand and finely chopped straw when he was digging a pit in his cellar to preserve carrots. Gee, that would taste good. This Tab doesn't taste real. He would like a glass of Calvados and he would like one of those big rugs the Thugs made after their rehabilitation. Those men changed their lives. From stranglers, they became weavers. Oh, G. has always wanted one of those rugs! What a conversation piece!

THE CHILDREN ARE flying around like dervishes. Crazy kids. G. stares at them, absorbed, intent. His jaw begins to ache. He lights a cigarette, smokes, coughs, yawns, laughs. Jesus never laughed. *Poor guy*, G. thinks. A small boy in silk shorts, a shirt covered with arcane lettering and black roller skates with huge green wheels floats up to the wall and crashes into it. G. laughs. *I know what that feels like*, he thinks. *That tree outside Fontainebleau did not move one inch. Be careful*, he shouts to the small boy, laughing. *Or you'll be like me, a bit of live meat in a clean bed.* He is asked to leave.

G. WALKS ALONG the beach. *What I need is to get into the ocean*, he thinks. But there is only the Gulf. He's taking it all in. *I'm in Florida!* he thinks. His great shaven dome gleams in the sun. He approaches the water, swishes his right foot in it. It's tepid, the water. *I'm not being spontaneous enough*, G. worries. *I should just run right in, catch a wave, bodysurf back out. Or maybe I should just do a little skim-boarding in the shallows.* Under his overcoat he wears a pair of red shorts, not Nantucket reds but close to the color of Nantucket reds. When G.'s granny was dying, she said to G.: *In Life Never Do As Others Do.* On her deathbed, her last words, imagine! Saying that to a little kid.

G. SITS ON the shore. It is January, G. was born in January. It's getting dark. *Uh-oh*, G. thinks. Down the beach comes a black carriage drawn by an old horse guided by a drunken coachman. *This is very familiar*, G. thinks. His dark eyes glitter as he regards the spectacle. Everything is exactly right. The coachman is ignorant and disheveled, the horse is mistreated and spiritless, the carriage is in need of repair. *An exact cosmic actualization of my most favorite metaphor*, G. exclaims with delight. *Here!* The carriage stops in front of G. There is *no way* G. is going to get into that carriage. Nonchalantly, he bends down and picks up a little piece of coral and sails it out over the water. Plip Plip Plip Plip PlipPlipPlip it goes. Cursing, the coachman urges his horse onward. The horse doesn't move. The coachman climbs down from the carriage and starts beating the horse, punching him in the neck, kicking him in the ribs. Suddenly a German rushes out from behind a clump of sea oats and stays the violent coachman's hand. It is Nietzsche, Friedrich Nietzsche! He throws his arms around the horse's head and goes insane on the spot. No question about it, completely insane. He is taken off, babbling, in the broken-down carriage. G. looks after them, startled, but then remembers that it *is* January. *Nice forehead*, he has to admit. G. is alone once more on the darkening shore. Completely alone. But nothing has been lost. Nothing.

Damon Runyon

THE STONE CRAB

ONE OF THE more regrettable circumstances attendant upon the tourist invasion of Dade County, Florida, of recent Winters, was the discovery by visitors of the stone crab.

The home folks down in Dade County, Florida, have long esteemed the stone crab the greatest of native delicacies and can remember when they were so numerous that a man could dip a foot anywhere in Biscayne Bay and come up with a stone crab hanging on each toe. Or lacking the energy to dunk a pedal he could buy more stone crabs for a few bits than a horse could lug.

Since the Winter visitors got on to the stone crab, however, the crustaceans have become scarce and costly. They now sell by the

---

Damon Runyon's short stories in Guys and Dolls *defined 1930s Broadway. But his newspaper column, "The Brighter Side," exposed his deepest feelings, like his love for stone crab. This excerpt is from the menu of Joe's Stone Crab, Miami Beach.*

karat. They are so expensive that the home folks are inclined to leave them on their menus. The visitors eat more of the stone crab nowadays and this is all the more deplorable when you reflect that stone crabs are really too good for visitors. A certificate of at least four years residence in Dade County should be required of every person desiring stone crabs.

The stone crab is an ornery looking critter that hangs out around the Florida Keys and nowhere else in the world. It is a sucker for a trap baited with fish. It bears some resemblance to the California crab, but is cooked and served differently and the taste is also different. Occasionally a Californian from up around San Francisco drifts into Dade County, Florida, and goes against stone crabs and right away he wants to go out in the kitchen and start an argument with the chef on the basis that the California cracked crab tastes better.

This is where we would not care to take sides. We always bear in mind the experience of a New York fellow who stepped between a Californian and a New Yorker who were arguing the respective merits of the California cracked crab and the Florida stone crab. The poor soul incautiously ventured the statement that the northern crab tastes better than either and he got slugged from two directions.

The stone crab is much larger than the northern crab and has a shell harder than a landlord's heart. In places in Dade County where stone crabs are served, the shell is cracked with a large wooden mallet before being set before the customer. Only the huge claws of the stone crab contain the edible meat. The body is waste, but when the live crab is weighed the body is included in the total poundage and the buyer pays by the pound.

The stone crab is cooked by boiling. A lot of people have tried to think up better ways, but boiling is best. It is served cold with hot melted butter with a dash of lemon in it on the side. Probably the right place in which to eat stone crabs would be the bathtub. The fingers are used in toying with them. Some high-toned folks use those little dinky oyster forks, but the fingers are far speedier and more efficient.

In Dade County prior to 1920, no one bothered much with stone crabs as an article of diet. Then the late Jim Allison, of Indianapolis, one of the builders of Miami Beach, who had an aquarium on the shores of Biscayne Bay loaded with aquatic fauna of various kinds, imported a Harvard professor to study and classify the local fish and one day this professor saw some boys with a bunch of stone crabs.

He wanted to know what they were going to do with them, and they said they were going to throw them away. The professor said that was bad judgement as the crabs were good eating, and somebody tried them and found he was right as rain. Biscayne Bay was full of stone crabs at that time, but harbor blasting and dredging chased them away and the great crabbing grounds are now to the south of Dade County, along the Keys, a Key being just a small island.

There is a restaurant at the south of Miami Beach known as Joe's which specializes in stone crabs. Joe's, the oldest and most famous restaurant on the beach, is conducted by Joe Weiss, whose father established the place around 1919. Weiss has his own boats operating during the stone crab season which runs from October 15 to May 15 and this gives him a big edge over the other restaurant men on the crabs. He uses as high as a thousand pounds of crabs a day.

The stone crab of Dade County seems to be the morro crab of Cuba with a Spanish accent. They are both ugly enough to enjoy some kinship. It is the look of the stone crab that has deterred many a Winter visitor to Dade County from eating it—many, but not enough to suit those of us who view the inroads of the visitors on the crab supply with genuine alarm.

John D. MacDonald

The Long, Lavender Look

LATE APRIL. TEN o'clock at night. Hustling south on Florida 112 through the eastern section of Cypress County, about twenty miles from the intersection of 112 and the Tamiami Trail.

So maybe I was pushing old Miss Agnes along a little too fast. Narrow macadam. Stars above, and some wisps of ground mist below. But not much of it, and not often.

The big tires of the old blue Rolls pickup rumbled along the roughened surface. Big black drainage canal paralleling the road on the left side. Now and then an old wooden bridge arching across the canal to serve one of the shacky little frame houses tucked back in the swamp and skeeter country. No traffic. And it had been a long long

---

John D. MacDonald is the author of over 50 best-selling novels, including Cape Fear *and* The Brass Cupcake. *Twenty-two of his novels—including* The Long, Lavender Look (1970)—*star his Floridian boat-bum/vigilante Travis McGee.*

day, and I was anxious to get back to Lauderdale, to Bahia Mar, to *The Busted Flush*, to a long hot shower and a long cold drink and a long deep sleep.

I had the special one-mile spots turned on. They are bracketed low on the massive front bumper. Essential for fast running through the balmy Florida nights on the straight narrow back roads, because her own headlights are feeble and set too high.

Meyer, beside me, was in a semidoze. We'd been to the wedding of the daughter of an old friend, at the fish camp he owns on Lake Passkokee. It is a very seldom thing to be able to drink champagne, catch a nine-pound bass, and kiss a bride all within the same hour. Meyer had been giving me one of his lectures on the marital condition.

So I was whipping along, but alert for the wildlife. I hate to kill a raccoon. Urban Florida is using the rabies myth to justify wiping them out, with guns, traps, and poison. The average raccoon is more affable, intelligent, and tidy than the average meathead who wants them eliminated, and is usually a lot better looking.

It is both sad and ironic that the areas where the raccoon are obliterated are soon overrun with snakes.

I was alert for any reflection of my headlights in animal eyes in the darkness of the shoulders of the road, for any dark shape moving out into the long reach of the beams.

But I wasn't prepared for the creature of the night that suddenly appeared out of the blackness, heading from left to right, at a headlong run. At eighty, you are covering about a hundred and twenty feet per second. She was perhaps sixty feet in front of the car when I first saw her. So half of one second later, when I last saw her, she was maybe ten inches from the flare of my front right fender, and that ten inches was the product of the first effect of my reaction time. Ten inches of living space instead of that bone-crunching, flesh-smashing thud which, once heard, lingers forever in the part of the mind where echoes live.

And I became very busy with Miss Agnes. She put her back end onto the left shoulder, and then onto the right shoulder. The swinging headlights showed me the road once in a while. I could not risk touching the brake. This was the desperate game of steering with the skid each time, and feeding her a morsel of gas for traction whenever she was coming back into alignment with the highway. I knew I had it whipped, and knew that each swing was less extreme.

Then a rear tire went and I lost her for good. The back end came around and there was a shriek of rubber, crashing of brush, a bright cracking explosion inside my skull, and I was vaguely aware of being underwater, disoriented, tangled in strange objects, and aware of the fact that it was not a very good place to be. I did not feel any alarm. Just a mild distaste, an irritation with my situation.

Something started grabbing at me and I tried to make it let go. Then I was up in the world of air again, and being dragged up a slope, coughing and gagging, thinking that it was a lot more comfortable back under the water.

"You all right, Trav? Are you all right?"

I couldn't answer until I could stop retching and coughing. "I don't know yet."

Meyer helped me up. I stood, sopping wet, on the gravelly shoulder and flexed all the more useful parts and muscles. There was a strange glow in the black water. I realized Miss Agnes's lights were still on, and she had to be ten feet under. The light went off abruptly as the water shorted her out.

I found a couple of tender places where I had hit the wheel and the door, and a throbbing lump on my head, dead center, just above the hairline.

"And how are you?" I asked Meyer.

"I'm susceptible to infections of the upper respiratory tract, and I'd like to lose some weight. Otherwise, pretty good."

"In a little while I think I'm going to start being glad you came along for the ride."

"Maybe you'd have gotten out by yourself."

"I don't think so."

"I'd rather think so. Excuse me. Otherwise I have to share the responsibility for all your future acts."

"Do I ever do anything you wouldn't do, Meyer?"

"I could make a list?"

That was when the reaction hit. A nice little case of the yips and shudders. And a pair of macaroni knees. I sat down gently on the shoulder of the road, wrapped my arms around my legs, and rested my forehead on my wet knees.

"Are you all right, Trav?"

"You keep asking me that. I think I will be very fine and very dandy. Maybe five or ten minutes from now."

It seemed very very quiet. The bugs were beginning to find us. A night bird yawped way back in the marshland. Vision had adjusted to the very pale wash of starlight on the road and on the black glass surface of the drainage canal.

Miss Agnes was down there, resting on her side, facing in the direction from which we had come, driver's side down. Sorry, old lady. We gave it a good try, and damned near made it. Except for the tire going, you did your usual best. Staunch, solid, and, in a very dignified way, obedient. Even in extremis, you managed to keep from killing me.

I got up and gagged and tossed up half a cup of swamp water. Before he could ask me again, I told Meyer I felt much improved. But irritable.

"What I would dearly like to do," I said, "is go back and find that moronic female, raise some angry welts on her rear end, and try to teach her to breathe under water."

"Female?"

"You didn't see her?" I asked him.

"I was dreaming that I, personally, Meyer, had solved the gold drain dilemma, and I was addressing all the gnomes of Zurich. Then I woke up and we were going sideways. I found the sensation unpleasant."

"She ran across in front of us. Very close. If I hadn't had time to begin to react, I'd have boosted her with the right front fender, and she would be a piece of dead meat in a treetop back there on the right side of the road."

"Please don't tell me something."

"Don't tell you what?"

"Tell me she was a shrunken old crone. Or tell me she looked exactly like Arnold Palmer. Or even tell me you didn't get a good look at her. Please?"

I closed my eyes and reran the episode on my little home screen inside my head. Replay is always pretty good. It has to be. Lead the kind of life where things happen very quickly and very unexpectedly, and sometimes lethally, and you learn to keep the input wide open. It improves the odds.

"I'd peg her at early to middle twenties. Black or dark brown hair, that would maybe have been shoulder length if she wasn't running like hell. She had some kind of ribbon or one of those plastic bands on her hair. Not chunky, but solid. Impression of good health. Not very tall. Hmm. Barefoot? I don't really know. Maybe not, unless she's got feet like rhino hide. Wearing a short thing, patterned. Flower pattern? Some kind of pattern. Light-weight material. Maybe one of those mini-nightgowns. Open down the front and at the throat, so that it was streaming out behind her, like her dark hair. Naked, I think. Maybe a pair of sheer little briefs, but it could have been just white hide in contrast to the suntanned rest of her. Caught a glint of something on one wrist. Bracelet or watch strap. She was running well, running hard, getting her knees up, getting a good swing of her arms into it. A flavor of being scared, but not in panic. And not winded. Mouth closed. I think she had her jaw clamped. Determination. She was running like hell, but away from something, not after it. If she started a tenth of a second earlier, we'd be rolling east on the Trail by now. A tenth of a second later, and she'd be one dead young lady, and I could have racked Miss Agnes up a little more solidly, and maybe you or I or both of us would be historical figures. Sorry, Meyer. Young and interestingly put together, and perhaps even pretty."

He sighed. "McGee, have you ever wondered if you don't emit some sort of subliminal aroma, a veritable dog whistle among scents? I have read about the role that some scent we cannot even detect plays in the reproductive cycle of the moth. The scientists spread some of it on a tree limb miles from nowhere, and within the hour there were hundreds upon hundreds of . . . . "

He stopped as we both saw the faraway, oncoming lights. It seemed a long time before they were close enough for us to hear the drone of the engine. We stepped into the roadway and began waving our arms. The sedan faltered, and then the driver floored it and it slammed on by, accelerating. Ohio license. We did not look like people anybody would want to pick up on a dark night on a very lonely road.

"I was wearing my best smile," Meyer said sadly.

We discussed probabilities and possibilities. Twenty miles of empty road from there to the Tamiami Trail. And, in the other direction, about ten miles back to a crossroads with darkened store, darkened gas station. We walked back and I tried to pinpoint the place where the girl had come busting out into the lights, but it was impossible to read black skid marks on black macadam. No lights from any house on either side.

No little wooden bridge. No driveway. Wait for a ride and get chewed bloody. So start the long twenty miles and hit the first place that shows a light. Or maybe get a ride. A remote maybe.

Before we left we marked Miss Agnes's watery resting place by wedging a long heavy broken limb down into the mud and jamming an aluminum beer can onto it. Miracle metal. Indestructible. Some day the rows of glittering cans will be piled so high beside the roads that they will hide the billboards which advertise the drinkables which come in the aluminum cans.

Just before we left I had the final wrench of nausea and tossed up the final cup of ditchwater. We kept to the middle of the road and found a fair pace. By the time our shoes stopped making sloppy noises, we were swinging along in good style.

"Four miles an hour," Meyer said. "If we could do it without taking a break, five hours to the Tamiami Trail. By now it must be quarter to eleven. Quarter to four in the morning. But we'll have to take a few breaks. Add an hour and a half, let's say. Hmm. Five-fifteen."

Scuff and clump of shoes on the blacktop. Keening orchestras of tree toads and peepers. *Gu-roomp* of a bullfrog. Whine song of the hungry mosquito keeping pace, then a *whish* of the fly whisk improvised from a leafy roadside weed. Jet going over, too high to pick out the lights. Startled caw and panic-flapping of a night bird working the canal for his dinner. And once, the eerie, faraway scream of a Florida panther.

The second car barreled by at very high speed, ignoring us completely, as did an old truck heading north a few minutes later.

But a good old Ford pickup truck came clattering and banging along, making the anguished sounds of fifteen years of bad roads, heavy duty, neglect, and a brave start on its second or third trip around the speedometer. One headlight was winking on and off. It slowed down as if to stop a little beyond us. We were over on the left shoulder. I could see a burly figure at the wheel.

When it was even with us, there was a flame-wink at the driver's window, a great flat unechoing bang, and a pluck of wind an inch or less from my right ear. When you've been shot at before, even only once, that distinctive sound which you can hear only when you are right in front of the muzzle, is unmistakable. And if you have heard that sound several times, and you are still alive, it means that your reflexes are in good order. I had hooked Meyer around the waist with my left arm and I was charging like a lineman when I heard the second bang. We tumbled down the weedy slope into the muddy shallows of the canal. The truck went creaking and thumping along, picking up laborious speed, leaving a smell of cordite and hot half-burned oil in the night air.

"Glory be!" said Meyer.

We were half in the water. We pulled ourselves up the slope like clumsy alligators.

"They carry guns and they get smashed and they shoot holes in the road signs," I said.

"And they scare hitchhikers and laugh like anything?"

"The slug was within an inch of my ear, old friend."

"How could you know that?"

"They make a little kind of thupping sound, which would come at the same time as the bang, so if it was further away from my ear, I wouldn't have heard it. If he'd fired from a hundred yards away, you'd have heard it, too. And if it had been a sniper with a rifle from five hundred yards, we'd have heard a whirr and a thup and then the shot."

"Thank you, Travis, for the information I hope never to need."

He started to clamber the rest of the way up and I grabbed him and pulled him back. "Rest awhile, Meyer."

"Reason?"

"If we assume it is sort of a hobby, like jacking deer, he is rattling on out of our lives, singing old drinking songs. If it was a real and serious intent, for reasons unknown, he will be coming back. We couldn't find where the young lady busted out of the brush, but we didn't have headlights. He does, and he may be able to see where we busted the weeds. So now we move along the slope here about thirty feet to the south and wait some more."

We made our move, found a more gradual slope where we didn't have to keep our feet in the water. Settled down, and heard the truck coming back. Evidently he had to go some distance to find a turnaround place. Heard him slow down. Saw lights against the grasses a couple of feet above our heads. Lights moved on beyond us, the truck slowing down to a walk. Stopped. The engine idled raggedly. I wormed up to where I could part the grasses and look at the rear end of the truck. Feeble light shone on a mud-smeared Florida plate. Couldn't read any of it. Engine and lights were turned off. Right-hand wheels were on the shoulder. Silence.

I eased back down, mouth close to Meyer's ear. "He better not have a flashlight."

Silence. The bugs and frogs gradually resumed their night singing. I held my breath, straining to hear any sound. Jumped at the sudden rusty bang of the truck door.

I reached cautiously down, fingered up a daub of mud, smeared my face, wormed up the slope again. Could make out the truck, an angular shadow in the starlight, twenty feet away.

"Orville! You hear me, Orville?" A husky shout, yet secretive. A man shouting in a whisper. "You all alone now, boy. I kilt me that big Hutch, right? Dead or close to it, boy. Answer me, Orville, damn you to hell!"

I did not like the idea of announcing that there was nobody here named Orville. Or Hutch.

Long silence. "Orville? We can make a deal. I got to figure you can hear me. You wedge that body down good, hear? Stake it into the mud. Tomorrow you call me on the telephone, hear? We can set up a place we can meet and talk it all out, someplace with enough people nearby neither of us has to feel edgy."

I heard a distant, oncoming motor sound. The truck door slammed again. Sick slow whine of the starter under the urging of the fading battery. Sudden rough roar, backfire, lights on, and away he went. Could be two of them, one staying behind and waiting, crouched down on the slope, aching to put a hole in old Orville.

I told Meyer to stay put. Just as the northbound sedan went by, soon to overtake the truck, I used the noise and wind of passage to cover my sounds as I bounded up and ran north along the shoulder. I had kept my eyes squeezed tightly shut to protect my night vision. If anyone were in wait, I hoped they had not done the same. I dived over the slope just where the truck had been parked, caught myself short of the water. Nobody.

Climbed back up onto the road. Got Meyer up onto the road. Made good time southward, made about three hundred yards, stopping three or four times to listen to see if the truck was easing back with the lights out.

Found a reasonably open place on the west side of the road, across from the canal. Worked into the shadows, pushed through a thicket. Found open space under a big Australian pine. Both of us sat on the springy bed of brown needles, backs against the bole of the big tree. Overhead a mockingbird was sweetly, fluently warning all other mockingbirds to stay the hell away from his turf, his nest, his lady, and his kids.

Meyer stopped breathing as audibly as before and said, "It is very unusual to be shot at on a lonely road. It is very unusual to have a girl run across a lonely road late at night. I would say we'd covered close to four miles from the point where Agnes sleeps. The truck came from that direction. Perfectly reasonable to assume some connection."

"Don't upset me with logic."

"A deal has a commercial implication. The marksman was

cruising along looking for Orville and Hutch. He did not want to make a deal with both of them. He knew they were on foot, knew they were heading south. Our sizes must be a rough match. And it is not a pedestrian area."

"And Hutch," I added, "was the taller, and the biggest threat, and I moved so fast he thought he'd shot me in the face. And, if he had a good, plausible, logical reason for killing Hutch, he wouldn't have asked Orville to stuff the body into the canal and stake it down."

"And," said Meyer, "were I Orville, I would be a little queasy about making a date with that fellow."

"Ready to go?"

"We should, I guess, before the mosquitoes remove the rest of the blood."

"And when anything comes from any direction, we flatten out in the brush on this side of the road."

"I think I will try and enjoy the walk, McGee."

"But your schedule is way the hell off."

So we walked. And were euphoric and silly in the jungly night. Being alive is like fine wine, when you have damned near drowned and nearly been shot in the face. Perhaps a change of angle of one degree at the muzzle would have put that slug through the bridge of my nose. So we swung along and told fatuous jokes and old lies and sometimes sang awhile.

Nathaniel Hawthorne

Ponce de Leon's Fountain of Youth

"Did you never hear of the fountain of youth?" he inquired of his guests, "which Ponce de Léon, the Spanish adventurer, went in search of?"

"Did Ponce de Léon ever find it?" asked the Widow Wycherly.

"No," answered Dr. Heidegger, "for he never sought for it in the right place. The famous Fountain of Youth is situated in the southern part of the peninsula of Florida. Its source is overshadowed by several gigantic magnolias, which, though numberless centuries old, have been kept fresh as violets by the virtues of this wonderful

Nathaniel Hawthorne's classic novels of early America include The House of Seven Gables *and* The Scarlet Letter. *Hawthorne was fascinated by Ponce de Leon's search for the fountain of youth—in this 1850 piece, he imagines the philosopher Heidegger (a fictional character, no relation to Martin) amusing his dinner guests with a strange tale.*

water. An acquaintance of mine, knowing my curiosity in such matters, has sent me some of it which you see in this vase. All of you, my respected friends, are welcome to as much of this admirable fluid as may restore you to the bloom of youth. For my own part having had so much trouble in growing old, I am in no hurry to grow young again."

He accordingly proceeds to administer to his four aged friends several draughts of the water; which restore them, first to advanced middle age, then to the prime of life, and lastly to the first glow and vigour of early youth. Instantly they begin to display all the vanities and follies they had practiced sixty years before. The three gentlemen dispute and quarrel, first angrily and then furiously, for the favour of the lady. She practices all the coquetry of her girlhood, inciting to a still higher pitch the passions of her suitors, until in their struggles they overthrow the vase, and spill the water. This, it is found, is very transient in its effects. The four rejuvenescents soon begin to grow old again, and clamorously entreat the doctor to procure some more of the wonderful water; failing which they resolve straightaway to set out for Florida, and quaff morning, noon and night, of the Fountain of Youth. The doctor's final remarks are too fine to be omitted.

"So, the Water of Youth is all lavished on the ground. Well, I bemoan it not, for if the fountain gushed at my door step, I would not stoop to bathe my lips in it—no, not though its delirium were for years instead of moments! Such is the lesson ye have taught me!"

Joan Didion

MIAMI

DURING THE SPRING when I began visiting Miami all of Florida
was reported to be in drought, with dropping water tables and
unfilled aquifers and SAVE WATER signs, but drought, in a part of the
world which would be in its natural state a shelf of porous oolitic
limestone covered most of the year by a shallow sheet flow of fresh
water, proved relative. During this drought the city of Coral Gables
continued, as it had every night since 1924, to empty and refill its
Venetian Pool with fresh unchlorinated water, 820,000 gallons a day
out of the water supply and into the storm sewer. There was less
water than there might have been in the Biscayne Aquifer but there
was water everywhere above it. There were rains so hard that wind-

---

In her 1960s and 1970s books, Slouching Toward Bethlehem *and* The White
Album, *Joan Didion mourned the death of California and the American Dream.
In her recent volumes, she has explored other regions, notably in 1987's* Miami, *a
jarring study of a U.S. city on the fringe of Latin America.*

shield wipers stopped working and cars got swamped and stalled on I-95. There was water roiling and bubbling over the underwater lights in decorative pools. There was water sluicing off the six-story canted window at the Omni, a hotel from which it was possible to see, in the Third World way, both the slums of Overtown and those island houses with the Universal Security and Ready Access to the Ocean, equally wet. Water plashed off banana palms, water puddled on flat roofs, water streamed down the CARNE U.S. GOOD & U.S. STAN- DARD signs on Flagler Street. Water rocked the impounded drug boats which lined the Miami River and water lapped against the causeways on the bay. I got used to the smell of incipient mildew in my clothes. I stuffed Kleenex in wet shoes and stopped expecting them to dry.

A certain liquidity suffused everything about the place. Causeways and bridges and even Brickell Avenue did not stay put but rose and fell, allowing the masts of ships to glide among the marble and glass facades of the unleased office buildings. The buildings themselves seemed to swim free against the sky: there had grown up in Miami during the recent money years an architecture which appeared to have slipped its moorings, a not inappropriate style for a terrain with only a provisional claim on being land at all. Surfaces were reflective, opalescent. Angles were oblique, intersecting to dis- orienting effect. The Arquitectonica office, which produced the cele- brated glass condominium on Brickell Avenue with the fifty-foot cube cut from its center, the frequently photographed "sky patio" in which there floated a palm tree, a Jacuzzi, and a lipstick-red spiral staircase, accompanied its elevations with crayon sketches, all moons and starry skies and airborne maidens, as in a Chagall. Skidmore, Owings and Merrill managed, in its Southeast Financial Center, the considerable feat of rendering fifty-five stories of polished gray granite incorporeal, a sky-blue illusion.

Nothing about Miami was exactly fixed, or hard. Hard consonants were missing from the local speech patterns, in English as well as in Spanish. Local money tended to move on hydraulic verbs: when it was not being washed it was being diverted, or channeled through Mexico, or turned off in Washington. Local stories tended to turn on underwater plot points, submerged snappers: on unsoundable extradition proceedings in the Bahamas, say, or fluid connections with the Banco Nacional de Colombia. I recall trying to touch the bottom of one such story in the *Herald*, about six hand grenades which had just been dug up in the bay-front backyard of a Biscayne Boulevard pawnbroker who had been killed in his own bed a few years before, shot at close range with a .25-caliber automatic pistol.

There were some other details on the surface of this story, for example the wife who fired the .25-caliber automatic pistol and the nineteen-year-old daughter who was up on federal weapons charges and the flight attendant who rented the garage apartment and said that the pawnbroker had collected "just basic things like rockets, just defused things," but the underwater narrative included, at last sounding, the Central Intelligence Agency (with which the pawnbroker was said to have been associated), the British intelligence agency MI6 (with which the pawnbroker was also said to have been associated), the late Anastasio Somoza Debayle (whose family the pawnbroker was said to have spirited into Miami shortly before the regime fell in Managua), the late shah of Iran (whose presence in Panama was said to have queered an arms deal about which the pawnbroker had been told), Dr. Josef Mengele (for whom the pawnbroker was said to be searching), and a Pompano Beach resident last seen cruising Miami in a cinnamon-colored Cadillac Sedan de Ville and looking to buy, he said for the Salvadoran insurgents, a million rounds of ammunition, thirteen thousand assault rifles, and "at least a couple" of jeep-mounted machine guns.

IN THIS MOOD Miami seemed not a city at all but a tale, a romance of the tropics, a kind of waking dream in which any possibility could and would be accommodated. The most ordinary morning, say at the courthouse, could open onto the distinctly lurid. "I don't think he came out with me, that's all," I recall hearing someone say one day in an elevator at the Miami federal courthouse. His voice had kept rising. "What happened to all that stuff about how next time, he gets twenty keys, he could run wherever-it-is-Idaho, now he says he wouldn't know what to do with five keys, what is this shit?" His companion had shrugged. We had continued in silence to the main floor. Outside one courtroom that day a group of Colombians, the women in silk shirts and Chanel necklaces and Charles Jourdan suede pumps, the children in appliquéd dresses from Baby Dior, had been waiting for the decision in a pretrial detention hearing, one in which the government was contending that the two defendants, who between them lived in houses in which eighty-three kilos of cocaine and a million-three in cash had been found, failed to qualify as good bail risks.

"That doesn't make him a longtime drug dealer," one of the two defense lawyers, both of whom were Anglo and one of whom drove a Mercedes 380 SEL with the license plate DEFENSE, had argued about the million-three in cash. "That could be one transaction." Across the hall that day closing arguments were being heard in a boat case, a "boat case" being one in which a merchant or fishing vessel has been boarded and drugs seized and eight or ten Colombian crew members arrested, the kind of case in which pleas were typically entered so that one of the Colombians would get eighteen months and the others deported. There were never any women in Chanel neck-laces around a boat case, and the lawyers (who were usually hired and paid for not by the defendants but by the unnamed owner of the "load," or shipment) tended to be Cuban. "You had the great argu-ment, you got to give me some good ideas," one of the eight Cuban defense lawyers on this case joked with the prosecutor during a recess. "But you haven't heard my argument yet," another of the defense lawyers said. "The stuff about communism. Fabulous closing argument."

Just as any morning could turn lurid, any moment could turn final, again as in a dream. "I heard a loud, short noise and then there was just a plain moment of dullness," the witness to a shooting in a Miami Beach supermarket parking lot told the *Herald*. "There was no one around except me and two bagboys." I happened to be in the coroner's office one morning when autopsies were being performed on the bodies of two Mariels, shot and apparently pushed from a car on I-95 about nine the evening before, another plain moment of dullness. The story had been on television an hour or two after it happened: I had seen the crime site on the eleven o'clock news, and had not expected to see the victims in the morning. "When he came here in Mariel he stayed at our house but he didn't get along with my mom," a young girl was saying in the anteroom to one of the detectives working the case. "These two guys were killed together," the detective had pressed. "They probably knew each other."

"For sure," the young girl had said, agreeably. Inside the autopsy room the hands of the two young men were encased in the brown paper bags which indicated that the police had not yet taken what they needed for laboratory studies. Their flesh had the marbleized yellow look of the recently dead. There were other bodies in the room, in various stages of autopsy, and a young woman in a white coat taking eyes, for the eye bank. "Who are we going to start on next?" one of the assistant medical examiners was saying. "The fat guy? Let's do the fat guy."

It was even possible to enter the waking dream without leaving the house, just by reading the *Herald*. A Mariel named Jose "Coca-Cola" Yero gets arrested, with nine acquaintances, in a case involving 1,664 pounds of cocaine, a thirty-seven-foot Cigarette boat named *The Connection*, two Lamborghinis, a million-six in cash, a Mercedes 500 SEL with another $350,000 in cash in the trunk, one dozen Rolex watches color-coordinated to match Jose "Coca-Cola" Yero's wardrobe, and various houses in Dade and Palm Beach counties, a search of one of which turns up not just a photograph of Jose "Coca-Cola" Yero face down in a pile of white powder but also a framed poster of Al Pacino as Tony Montana, the Mariel who appears at a dramatic moment in *Scarface* face down in a pile of white powder. "They got swept up in the fast lane," a Metro-Dade narcotics detective advises the *Herald*. "The fast lane is what put this whole group in jail." A young woman in South Palm Beach goes out to the parking lot of her parents' condominium and gets into her 1979 Pontiac Firebird, opens the T-top, starts the ignition and loses four toes when the bomb goes off. "She definitely knows someone is trying to kill her," the sheriff's investigator tells the *Herald*. "She knew they were coming, but she didn't know when."

SURFACES TENDED TO dissolve here. Clear days ended less so. I recall an October Sunday when my husband and I were taken, by Gene Miller, a *Herald* editor who had won two Pulitzer Prizes for investigative reporting and who had access to season tickets exactly on the fifty-yard line at the Orange Bowl, to see the Miami Dolphins beat the Pittsburgh Steelers, 21-17. In the row below us the former Dolphin quarterback Earl Morrall signed autographs for the children who wriggled over seats to slip him their programs and steal surreptitious glances at his Super Bowl ring. A few rows back an Anglo teenager in sandals and shorts and a black T-shirt smoked a marijuana cigarette in full view of the Hispanic police officer behind him. Hot dogs were passed, and Coca-Cola spilled. Sony Watchmans were compared, for the definition on the instant replay. The NBC cameras dollied along the sidelines and the Dolphin cheerleaders kneeled on their white pom-poms and there was a good deal of talk about red dogging and weak secondaries and who would be seen and what would be eaten in New Orleans, come Super Bowl weekend.

The Miami on display in the Orange Bowl that Sunday afternoon would have seemed another Miami altogether, one with less weather and harder, more American surfaces, but by dinner we were slipping back into the tropical: in a virtually empty restaurant on top of a virtually empty condominium off Biscayne Boulevard, with six people at the table, one of whom was Gene Miller and one of whom was Martin Dardis, who as the chief investigator for the state attorney's office in Miami had led Carl Bernstein through the local angles on Watergate and who remained a walking data bank on CDs at the Biscayne Bank and on who called who on what payoff and on how to follow a money chain, we sat and we talked and we watched a storm break over Biscayne Bay. Sheets of warm rain washed down the big windows. Lightning began to fork somewhere around Bal Harbour. Gene Miller mentioned the Alberto Duque trial, then entering its fourth week at the federal courthouse, the biggest bank fraud case ever tried in the United States. Martin Dardis mentioned the ESM Government Securities collapse, just then breaking into a fraud case maybe bigger than the Duque.

The lightning was no longer forking now but illuminating the entire sky, flashing a dead strobe white, turning the bay fluorescent and the islands black, as if in negative. I sat and listened to Gene Miller and Martin Dardis discuss these old and new turns in the underwater narrative and I watched the lightning backlight the islands. During the time I had spent in Miami many people had mentioned, always as something extraordinary, something I should have seen if I wanted to understand Miami, the *Surrounded Islands* project executed in Biscayne Bay in 1983 by the Bulgarian artist Christo. *Surrounded Islands*, which had involved surrounding eleven islands with two-hundred-foot petals, or skirts, of pink polypropylene fabric, had been mentioned both by people who were knowledgeable about conceptual art and by people who had not before heard and could not then recall the name of the man who had surrounded the islands. All had agreed. It seemed that the pink had shimmered in the water. It seemed that the pink had kept changing color, fading and reemerging with the movement of the water and the clouds and the sun and the night lights. It seemed that this period when the pink was in the water had for many people exactly defined, as the backlit islands and the fluorescent water and the voices at the table were that night defining for me, Miami.

Ernest Hemingway

He did not take the bicycle but walked down the street. The moon was up now and the trees were dark against it, and he passed the frame houses with their narrow yards, light coming from the shuttered windows; the unpaved alleys, with their double rows of houses; Conch town, where all was starched, well-shuttered, virtue, failure, grits and boiled grunts, under-nourishment, prejudice, righteousness, interbreeding and the comforts of religion; the open-doored, lighted Cuban bolito houses, shacks whose only romance was their names; The Red House, Chicha's; the pressed stone church; its steeples sharp, ugly triangles against the moonlight; the

---

Ernest Hemingway, the master of terse dialogue, American realism, and general swashbuckling, spent much of his time roaming the globe. These travels were the grist for his best books: The Sun Also Rises, A Moveable Feast, *and* The Old Man and the Sea. *He lived in Key West for 12 years (1928-40) soaking up atmosphere for his classic* To Have and Have Not.

big grounds and the long, black-domed bulk of the convent, handsome in the moonlight; a filling station and a sandwich place, bright-lighted beside a vacant lot where a miniature golf course had been taken out; past the brightly lit main street with the three drug stores, the music store, the five Jew stores, three poolrooms, two barbershops, five beer joints, three ice cream parlors, the five poor and the one good restaurant, two magazine and paper places, four second-hand joints (one of which made keys), a photographer's, an office building with four dentists' offices upstairs, the big dime store, a hotel on the corner with taxis opposite; and across, behind the hotel, to the street that led to jungle town, the big unpainted frame house with lights and the girls in the doorway, the mechanical piano going, and a sailor sitting in the street; and then on back, past the back of the brick courthouse with its clock luminous at half-past ten, past the white-washed jail building shining in the moonlight, to the embowered entrance of the Lilac Time where motor cars filled the alley.

Seminole Tale

WHEN THE GREAT Spirit made the Earth, he created three men at the same time. All of the men were fair-complexioned, and one day the Great Spirit took them to a lake and ordered them to jump into the water. One immediately obeyed the command and, when he came out of the water, he was fairer than before. The second hesitated and when he jumped, the water was a bit muddy because of the first man's agitation of the water. When he climbed out, his skin had become copper-colored. The third, having waited until the water was quite disturbed and muddy, came from the water with his complexion changed to black.

The Native Americans living in Spanish Florida became known as the Seminoles ("those who camped away"). After the formation of the United States, the Seminoles' territory became a haven for runaway slaves and refugees from various tribes. They fought two wars against the U.S., and were finally defeated by Andrew Jackson. Today the Seminoles live on reservations in Florida and Oklahoma.

The Great Spirit then placed before the men three sealed packages. He wanted to compensate the black man, so he gave him first choice as to which package he wanted. He took each package and tested its weight, and figuring the heaviest would have the most valuable contents, chose it. The copper-colored man chose the next heaviest, and the lightest was left for the white man. When the packages were opened, the first contained spades, hoes, and other implements used in manual labor, thus the black man has been relegated to this type of existence.

The second package, the one chosen by the red man, was opened next. It contained fishing tackle and weapons for hunting and war. The red man, or Indian, was designated by the Great Spirit to live close to nature and gain his livelihood from hunting and fishing.

The white man was the last to open his package and in it he found pens, ink, and paper. He was given the implements to make books and to write the stories of his people.

Each was given a place on the earth to occupy and carry on the particular life-style he had chosen.

Dave Barry

THE WALT "YOU WILL HAVE FUN" DISNEY WORLD
THEMED SHOPPING COMPLEX AND RESORT COMPOUND

I'M AN EXPERT on visiting Disney World, because we live only four hours away, and according to my records we spend about three-fifths of our after-tax income there. Not that I'm complaining. You can't have a bad time at Disney World. It's not *allowed*. They have hidden electronic surveillance cameras everywhere, and if they catch you failing to laugh with childlike wonder, they lock you inside a costume representing a beloved Disney character such as Goofy and make you walk around in the Florida heat getting grabbed and leaped on by violently excited children until you have learned your lesson. Yes, Disney World is a "dream vacation," and here are some tips to help make it "come true" for you!

Dave Barry is a Pulitzer Prize-winning columnist for the Miami Herald. *His books include* Homes and Other Black Holes, Claw Your Way to the Top, *and* Dave Barry Turns 40. *This quick visit to Disney World is from his 1991 travelogue* Dave Barry's Only Travel Guide You'll Ever Need.

When to Go: The best time to go, if you want to avoid huge crowds, is 1962.

How to Get There: It's possible to fly, but if you want the total Disney World experience, you should drive there with a minimum of four hostile children via the longest possible route. If you live in Georgia, for example, you should plan a route that includes Oklahoma.

Once you get to Florida, you can't miss Disney World, because the Disney corporation owns the entire center of the state. Just get on any major highway, and eventually it will dead-end in a Disney parking area large enough to have its own climate, populated by large nomadic families who have been trying to find their cars since the Carter administration. Be sure to note carefully where you leave *your* car, because later on you may want to sell it so you can pay for your admission tickets.

But never mind the price; the point is that now you're finally *there*, in the ultimate vacation fantasy paradise, ready to have fun! Well, okay, you're not exactly there *yet*. First you have to wait for the parking-lot tram, driven by cheerful uniformed Disney employees, to come around and pick you up and give you a helpful lecture about basic tram-safety rules such as never fall out of the tram without coming to a full and complete stop.

But now the tram ride is over and it's time for fun! Right? Don't be an idiot. It's time to wait in line to buy admission tickets. Most experts recommend that you go with the 47-day pass, which will give you a chance, if you never eat or sleep, to visit *all* of the

Disney themed attractions, including The City of the Future, The Land of Yesterday, The Dull Suburban Residential Community of Sometime Next Month, Wet Adventure, Farms on Mars, The World of Furniture, Sponge Encounter, the Nuclear Flute Orchestra, Appliance Island, and the Great Underwater Robot Hairdresser Adventure, to name just a few.

Okay, you've taken out a second mortgage and purchased your tickets! Now, finally, it's time to . . . wait in line again! This time, it's for the monorail, a modern, futuristic transportation system that whisks you to the Magic Kingdom at nearly half the speed of a lawn tractor. Along the way cheerful uniformed Disney World employees will offer you some helpful monorail-safety tips such as never set fire to the monorail without first removing your personal belongings.

And now, at last, you're at the entrance to the Magic Kingdom itself! No more waiting in line for transportation! It's time to *wait in line to get in.* Wow! Look at all the *other* people waiting to get in! There are tour groups here with names like "Entire Population of Indiana." There sure must be some great attractions inside these gates!

And now you've inched your way to the front of the line, and the cheerful uniformed Disney employee is stamping your hand with a special invisible chemical that penetrates your nervous system and causes you to temporarily acquire the personality of a cow. "Moo!" you shout as you surge forward with the rest of the herd.

And now, unbelievably, you're actually inside the Magic Kingdom! At last! Mecca! You crane your head to see over the crowd around you, and with innocent childlike wonder you behold: *a much larger crowd.* Ha ha! You are having some kind of fun now!

And now you are pushing your way forward, thrusting other vacationers aside, knocking over their strollers if necessary, because little Jason wants to ride on Space Mountain. Little Jason has been talking about Space Mountain ever since Oklahoma, and by God you're going to take him on it, no matter how long the . . . My God! Can *this* be the line for Space Mountain? This line is so long that there are Cro-Magnon families at the front! Perhaps if you explain to little Jason that he could be a deceased old man by the time he gets on the actual ride, he'll agree to skip it and . . . NO! Don't scream, little Jason! We'll just purchase some official Mickey Mouse sleeping bags, and we'll stay in line as long as it takes! The hell with third grade! We'll just stand here and chew our cuds! Mooooo!

Speaking of education, you should be sure to visit Epcot Center, which features exhibits sponsored by large corporations showing you how various challenges facing the human race are being met and overcome thanks to the selfless efforts of large corporations. Epcot Center also features pavilions built by various foreign nations, where you can experience an extremely realistic simulation of what life in these nations would be like if they consisted almost entirely of restaurants and souvenir shops.

One memorable Epcot night my family and I ate at the German restaurant, where I had several large beers and a traditional German delicacy called "Bloatwurst," which is a sausage that can either be eaten or used as a tackling dummy. When we got out I felt like one of those snakes that eat a cow whole and then just lie around and digest it for a couple of months. But my son was determined to go on a new educational Epcot ride called "The Body," wherein you sit in a compartment that simulates what it would be like if you got inside a spaceship-like vehicle and got shrunk down to the size of a gnat and got injected inside a person's body.

I'll tell you what it's like: awful. You're looking at a screen showing an extremely vivid animated simulation of the human interior, which is not the most appealing way to look at a human unless you're attracted to white blood cells the size of motor homes. Meanwhile the entire compartment is bouncing you around violently, especially when you go through the aorta. "Never go through the aorta after eating German food," that is my new travel motto.

What gets me is, I waited in line for an *hour* to do this. I could have experienced essentially the same level of enjoyment merely by sticking my finger down my throat.

Which brings me to my idea for getting rich. No doubt you have noted that, in most amusement parks, the popularity of a ride is directly proportional to how horrible it is. There's hardly ever a line for nice, relaxing rides like the merry-go-round. But there will always be a huge crowd, mainly consisting of teenagers, waiting to go on a ride with a name like "The Dicer," where they strap people into what is essentially a giant food processor and turn it on and then phone the paramedics.

So my idea is to open up a theme park called "Dave World," which will have a ride called "The Fall of Death." This will basically be a 250-foot tower. The way it will work is, you climb to the top, a trapdoor opens up, and you splat onto the asphalt below like a bushel of late-summer tomatoes.

Obviously, for legal reasons, I couldn't let anybody actually *go* on this ride. There would be a big sign that said:

WARNING!

NOBODY CAN GO ON THIS RIDE.

THIS RIDE IS INVARIABLY FATAL,

THANK YOU.

But this would only make The Fall of Death more popular. Every teenager in the immediate state would come to Dave World just to stand in line for it.

Dave World would also have an attraction called "Parentland," which would have a sign outside that said: "Sorry, Kids! This Attraction Is for Mom 'n' Dad Only!" Inside would be a bar. For younger children, there would be "Soil Fantasy," a themed play area consisting of dirt or, as a special "rainy-day" bonus, mud.

I frankly can't see how Dave World could fail to become a huge financial success that would make me rich and enable me to spend the rest of my days traveling the world with my family. So the hell with it.

Seeing Other Attractions in the Disney World Area
YOU MUST BE very careful here. You must sneak out of Disney World in the dead of night, because the Disney people do *not* want

you leaving the compound and spending money elsewhere. If they discover that you're gone, cheerful uniformed employees led by Mickey Mouse's lovable dog Pluto, who will sniff the ground in a comical manner, will track you down. And when they catch you, it's *into the Goofy suit.*

So we're talking about a major risk, but it's worth it for some of the attractions around Disney World. The two best ones, as it happens, are right next to each other near a town called Kissimmee. One of them is the world headquarters of the Tupperware company, where you can take a guided tour that includes a Historic Food Containers Museum. I am not making this up.

I am also not making up Gatorland, which is next door. After entering Gatorland through a giant pair of pretend alligator jaws, you find yourself on walkways over a series of murky pools in which are floating a large number of alligators that appear to be recovering from severe hangovers, in the sense that they hardly ever move. You can purchase fish to feed them, but the typical Gatorland alligator will ignore a fish even if it lands directly on its head. Sometimes you'll see an alligator, looking bored, wearing three or four rotting, fly-encrusted fish, like some kind of High Swamp Fashion headgear.

This is very entertaining, of course, but the *real* action at Gatorland, the event that brings even the alligators to life, is the Assault on the Dead Chickens, which is technically known as the Gator Jumparoo. I am also not making this up. The way it works is, a large crowd of tourists gathers around a central pool, over which, suspended from wires, are a number of plucked headless chicken carcasses. As the crowd, encouraged by the Gatorland announcer, cheers wildly, the alligators lunge out of the water and rip the chicken carcasses down with their jaws. Once you've witnessed this impressive event, you will never again wonder how America got to be the country that it is today.

Elmore Leonard

LA BRAVA

HE FOUND MAURICE in 304, the guest suite facing the ocean, the
room filled with sunlight and old slipcovered furniture. Maurice
took the prints without comment, began studying them as he moved
toward the closed door to the bedroom. LaBrava came in, followed
him part way. He was anxious, but remembered to keep his voice low.

"Why didn't you tell me who she is?"

"I did tell you."

"That's Jean Shaw."

"I know it's Jean Shaw. I told you that last night."

"She's supposed to be an old friend—you couldn't even
think of her name."

"I like this one, the expression. She doesn't know where the

Elmore Leonard redefined the crime novel with best-selling classics such as Glitz,
Mr. Majestyk, 52 Pick-Up, *and* Get Shorty. *This humid excerpt is from*
LaBrava, *one of his many mysteries set in Florida.*

hell she is." Maurice looked up from the prints, eyes wide behind his glasses. "What're you talking about, I couldn't think of her name? Twenty years she's been Jeanie Breen. I told you she left the picture business to marry Jerry Breen, her husband. I remember distinctly telling you that."

"How is she?"

"Not suffering as much as I hoped."

"You bring her some breakfast?"

"What do you think this is, a hotel?" Maurice turned to the bedroom, paused and glanced back with his hand on the door. "Wait here." He went in and all LaBrava saw was the salmon-colored spread hanging off the end of the bed. The door closed again.

Wait. He moved to one of the front windows, stood with his hands resting on the air-conditioning unit. He thought he knew everything there was to know about time. Time as it related to waiting. Waiting on surveillance. Waiting in Mrs. Truman's living room. But time was doing strange things to him now. Trying to confuse him.

What he saw from the window was timeless, a Florida post card. The strip of park across the street. The palm trees in place, the sea grape. The low wall you could sit on made of coral rock and gray cement. And the beach. What a beach. A desert full of people resting, it was so wide. People out there with blankets and umbrellas. People in the green part of the ocean, before it turned deep blue. People so small they could be from any time. Turn the view around. Sit on the coral wall and look this way at the hotels on Ocean Drive and see back into the thirties. He could look at the hotels, or he could look at Maurice's photographs all over his apartment, be reminded of pictures in old issues of *Life* his dad had saved, and feel what it was like to have lived in that time, the decade before he was born, when times were bad but the trend, the look, was to be "modern."

Now another time frame was presenting pictures, from real life and from memory. A 1950s movie star with dark hair parted in the middle, pale pure skin, black pupils, eyes that stared with cool expressions, knowing something, never smiling except with dark secrets. The pictures brought back feelings from his early teens, when he believed the good guy in the movie was out of his mind to choose the other girl, the sappy one who cried and dried her eyes with her apron, when he could have had Jean Shaw.

There were no sounds from the other room. No warning.

The door opened before he was ready. Maurice came out and a moment later there she was in a navy blue robe, dark hair, the same dark hair parted in the middle though not as long as she used to wear it and he wasn't prepared. He hadn't thought of anything to say that would work as a simple act of recognition, acknowledgment.

Maurice was no help. Maurice said, "I'll be right back," and walked out, leaving him alone in the same room with Jean Shaw.

She moved past the floral slipcovered sofa to the other front window, not paying any attention to him. Like he wasn't there. He saw her profile again, the same one, the same slender nose, remembering its delicate outline, the soft, misty profile as she stood at the window in San Francisco staring at the Bay. Foghorn moaning in the background. *Deadfall.* The guy goes off the bridge in the opening scene and everybody thinks it's suicide except the guy's buddy, Robert Mitchum. Robert Mitchum finds out somebody else was on the bridge that night, at the exact same time. A girl . . .

He saw the movie—it had to have been twenty-five years ago, because he was in the ninth grade at Holy Redeemer, he was playing American Legion ball and he went to see the movie downtown after a game, a bunch of them went. She did look older. Not much though. She was still thin and her features, with that clean delicate look, always a little bored, they were the same. He remembered the way she would toss her hair, a gesture, and stare at the guy very calmly, lips slightly parted. Robert Mitchum was no dummy, he grabbed her every chance he had in *Deadfall*, before he ended up with the dead guy's wife. That was the only trouble with her movies. She was only grabbed once or twice before the good guy went back to Arleen Whalen or Joan Leslie. She would have to be at least fifty. Twelve years older than he was. Or maybe a little more.

He didn't want to sound dumb. Like the president of a fan club. *Miss Shaw, I think I saw every picture you were ever in.*

She said, without looking at him, "You don't happen to have a cigarette, do you?"

It was her voice. Soft but husky, with that relaxed, off-hand tone. A little like Patricia Neal's voice. Jean Shaw reminded him a little of Patricia Neal, except Jean Shaw was more the mystery-woman type. In movies you saw Jean Shaw at night, hardly ever outside during the day. Jean Shaw could not have played that part in *Hud* Patricia

Neal played. Still, they were somewhat alike.

"I can get you a pack," LaBrava said. He remembered the way she held a cigarette and the way she would stab it into an ashtray, one stab, and leave it.

"Maury said he'll bring some. We'll see."

"I understand you're old friends."

"We were. It remains to be seen if we still are. I don't know what I'm suppose to do here, besides stare at the ocean." She came away from the window to the sofa, finally looking at him as she said, "I can do that at home. I think it's the same ocean I've been looking at for the past . . . I don't know, round it off, say a hundred years."

Dramatic. But not too. With that soft husky sound, her trademark.

He said, "You were always staring at the ocean in *Deadfall*. I thought maybe it was like your conscience bothering you. Wondering where the guy was out there, in the water."

Jean Shaw was seated now, with the *Miami Herald* on her lap. She brought a pair of round, wire-framed glasses out of the robe and slipped them on. "That was *Nightshade*."

"You sound just like her, the part you played."

"Why wouldn't I?"

"I think in *Deadfall* you lured the guy out on the bridge. You were having an affair, then you tried to blackmail him . . . In *Nightshade* you poisoned your husband."

She hesitated, looking up at him, and said very slowly, "You know, I think you're right. Who was the guy in the bridge picture?"

"Robert Mitchum."

"Yes, you're right. Mitchum was in *Deadfall*. Let me think. Gig Young was in *Nightshade*."

"He was the insurance investigator," LaBrava said. "But I think he grew flowers, too, as a hobby."

"Everybody in the picture grew flowers. The dialogue, at times it sounded like we were reading seed catalogues." She began looking at the front page of the *Herald*. Within a few moments her eyes raised to him again.

"You remember those pictures?"

"I bet I've seen every picture you were in." There. It didn't sound too bad. She was still looking at him.

She said, "Really?" and slipped her glasses off to study him, maybe wondering if he was putting her on. "On television? The late show?"

"No, in movie theaters, the first time." He didn't want to get into ages, how old he had been, and said, "Then I saw some of them again later. I'm pretty sure about *Deadfall* and *Nightshade* because I saw 'em both in Independence, Missouri, just last year."

"What were you doing in Independence, Missouri?" With that quiet, easy delivery.

"It's a long story—I'll tell you sometime if you want. What I could never figure out was why you never ended up with the guy in the movie, the star."

She said, "I was the spider woman, why do you think? My role was to come between the lead and the professional virgin. But in the end he goes back to little June Allyson and I say, 'Swell.' If I'm not dead."

"In *Deadfall*," LaBrava said, "I remember I kept thinking if I was Robert Mitchum I still would've gone for you instead of the guy's wife, the widow."

"But I was in on the murder. I lured what's his name out on the bridge. Was it Tom Drake?"

"It might've been. The thing is, your part was always a downer. At least once in a while you should've ended up with the star."

"You can't have it both ways. I played Woman as Destroyer, and that gave me the lines. And I'd rather have the lines any day than end up with the star."

"Yeah, I can understand that."

"Someone said that the character I played never felt for a moment that love could overcome greed. The only time, I think, I was ever in a kitchen was in *Nightshade*, to make the cookies. You remember the kitchen, the mess? That was the tip-off I'm putting belladonna in the cookie batter. Good wives and virgins keep their kitchens neat."

"It was a nice touch," LaBrava said. "I remember he takes the cookies and a glass of milk out to the greenhouse and practically wipes out all of his plants in the death scene, grabbing something to hold onto. Gig Young was good in that. Another one, *Obituary*, I remember the opening scene was in a cemetery."

She looked up as he said it and stared at him for a moment.

"When did you see *Obituary?*"

"Long time ago. I remember the opening and I remember, I think Henry Silva was in it, he was your boyfriend."

She was still watching him. She seemed mildly amazed.

"You were married to a distinguished looking gray-haired guy. I can sorta picture him, but I don't remember his name."

"Go on."

"And I remember—I don't know if it was that picture or another one—you shot the bad guy. He looks at the blood on his hand, looks down at his shirt. He still can't believe it. But I don't remember what it was about. I can't think who the detective was either, I mean in *Obituary*. It wasn't Robert Mitchum, was it?"

She shook her head, thoughtful. "I'm not sure myself who was in it."

"He seems like a nice guy. Robert Mitchum."

She said, "I haven't seen him in years. I think the last time was at Harry Cohn's funeral." She paused and said, "Now there was a rotten son of a bitch, Harry Cohn, but I loved him. He ran Columbia. God, did he run it." She looked up at LaBrava. "I haven't been interviewed in years, either."

"Is that what this is like?"

"It reminds me. Sitting in a hotel room in a bathrobe, doing the tour. Harry would advise you how to act. 'Be polite, don't say *shit*, keep your fucking knees together and don't accept any drink offers from reporters—all they want is to get in your pants.' Where in the hell is Maurice?"

LaBrava glanced toward the door. "He said he'd be right back."

There was a silence. He had been in the presence of political celebrities and world figures. He had stood alone, from a few seconds to a few minutes, with Jimmy Carter, Nancy Reagan, George Bush's wife Barbara, Rosalynn Carter and Amy, not Sadat but Menachem Begin at Camp David, Teddy Kennedy a number of times, nameless Congressmen, Tip O'Neill was one, Fidel Castro in New York, Bob Hope . . . but he had never felt as aware of himself as he did now, in front of Jean Shaw in her blue bathrobe.

"I was trying to think," LaBrava said, "what your last movie was."

She looked up from the paper. "Let's see, I made *Let It Ride* at Columbia. Went to RKO for one called *Moon Dance*. A disaster . . ."

"The insane asylum."

"I quit right after that. I tested for a picture that was shot right around here, a lot of it at the Cardozo Hotel. I thought sure I was going to get the part. Rich widow professional virgin, my first good girl. But they gave it to Eleanor Parker. It didn't turn out to be that much of a part."

"Frank Sinatra and Edward G. Robinson," LaBrava said, impressing the movie star.

She said, "That's right, *A Hole in the Head*. Frank Capra, his first picture in I think seven years. I really wanted to work with him. I even came here on my own to find out what rich Miami Beach widows were like."

"I think you would've been too young."

"That's why Frank gave it to Eleanor Parker. Before that, half the scripts I read had Jane Greer's prints all over them." She said then, "No, the last one wasn't *Moon Dance*. I went back to Columbia—oh my God, yeah—to do *Treasure of the Aztecs*."

"*Treasure of the Aztecs*," LaBrava said, nodding. He had never heard of it.

"Farley Granger was Montezuma's bastard son. In the last reel I'm about to be offered up to the gods on top of a pyramid, have my heart torn out, but I'm rescued by Cortez's younger brother. Remember?"

"The star," LaBrava said. "I can't think who it was."

"Audie Murphy. I took the first flight I could get out of Durango and haven't made a picture since."

"I imagine a lot of people liked it though."

"You didn't see it, did you?"

"I guess that's one I missed. How many pictures did you make?"

"Sixteen. From '55 to '63."

He could think of four titles. Maybe five. "I might've missed a couple of the early ones too," LaBrava said, "but I saw all the rest. I have to tell you, whether it means anything to you or not, you were *good*."

Jean Shaw raised her eyes to his, giving him that cool, familiar look. "Which one was your favorite?"

Zora Neale Hurston

My Birthplace

LIKE THE DEAD-seeming, cold rocks, I have memories within that came out of the material that went to make me. Time and place have had their say.

So you will have to know something about the time and place where I came from, in order that you may interpret the incidents and directions of my life.

I was born in a Negro town. I do not mean by that the black back-side of an average town. Eatonville, Florida, is, and was at the time of my birth, a pure Negro town—charter, mayor, council, town marshal and all. It was not the first Negro community in America,

Zora Neale Hurston's 1942 volume, Dust Tracks on the Road *is an autobiographical account of growing up in Eatonville, Florida, America's first incorporated black town. In 1928, young Hurston moved to New York, where she graduated from Barnard and became instrumental in the Harlem Renaissance. Late in life, she moved back to Florida, where she worked as a maid.*

but it was the first to be incorporated, the first attempt at organized self-government on the part of Negroes in America.

Eatonville is what you might call hitting a straight lick with a crooked stick. The town was not in the original plan. It is a by-product of something else.

It all started with three white men on a ship off the coast of Brazil. They had been officers in the Union Army. When the bitter war had ended in victory for their side, they had set out for South America. Perhaps the post-war distress made their native homes depressing. Perhaps it was just that they were young, and it was hard for them to return to the monotony of everyday being after the excitement of military life, and they, like numerous other young men, set out to find new frontiers.

But they never landed in Brazil. Talking together on the ship, these three decided to return to the United States and try their fortunes in the unsettled country of South Florida. No doubt the same thing which had moved them to go to Brazil caused them to choose South Florida.

This had been dark and bloody country since the mid-1700's. Spanish, French, English, Indian, and American blood had been bountifully shed.

The last great struggle was between the resentful Indians and the white planters of Georgia, Alabama, and South Carolina. The strong and powerful Cherokees, aided by the conglomerate Seminoles, raided the plantations and carried off Negro slaves into Spanish-held Florida. Ostensibly they were carried off to be slaves to the Indians, but in reality the Negro men were used to swell the ranks of the Indian fighters against the white plantation owners. During lulls in the long struggle, treaties were signed, but invariably broken. The sore point of returning escaped Negroes could not be settled satisfactorily to either side. Who was an Indian and who was a Negro? The whites contended all who had Negro blood. The Indians contended all who spoke their language belonged to the tribe. Since it was an easy matter to teach a slave to speak enough of the language to pass in a short time, the question could never be settled. So the wars went on.

The names of Oglethorpe, Clinch and Andrew Jackson are well known on the white side of the struggle. For the Indians, Miccanopy, Billy Bow-legs and Osceola. The noble Osceola was only a sub-chief, but he came to be recognized by both sides as the ablest of them all. Had he not been captured by treachery, the struggle would have lasted much longer than it did. With an offer of friendship, and a new rifle (some say a beautiful sword) he was lured to the fort seven miles outside of St. Augustine, and captured. He was confined in sombre Fort Marion that still stands in that city, escaped, was recaptured, and died miserably in the prison of a fort in Beaufort, South Carolina. Without his leadership, the Indian cause collapsed. The Cherokees and most of the Seminoles, with their Negro adherents, were moved west. The beaten Indians were moved to what is now Oklahoma. It was far from the then settlements of the whites. And then too, there seemed to be nothing there that white people wanted, so it was a good place for Indians. The wilds of

Florida heard no more clash of battle among men.

The sensuous world whirled on in the arms of ether for a generation or so. Time made and marred some men. So into this original hush came the three frontier-seekers who had been so intrigued by its prospects that they had turned back after actually arriving at the coast of Brazil without landing. These young men were no poor, refuge-seeking, wayfarers. They were educated men of family and wealth.

The shores of Lake Maitland were beautiful, probably one reason they decided to settle there, on the northern end where one of the old forts—built against the Indians, had stood. It had been commanded by Colonel Maitland, so the lake and the community took their names in memory of him. It was Mosquito County then and the name was just. It is Orange County now for equally good reason. The men persuaded other friends in the north to join them, and the town of Maitland began to be in a great rush.

Negroes were found to do the clearing. There was the continuous roar of the crashing of ancient giants of the lush woods, of axes, saws and hammers. And there on the shores of Lake Maitland rose stately houses, surrounded by beautiful grounds. Other settlers flocked in from upper New York State, Minnesota and Michigan, and Maitland became a center of wealth and fashion. In less then ten years, the Plant System, later absorbed into the Atlantic Coast Line Railroad, had been persuaded to extend a line south through Maitland, and the private coaches of millionaires and other dignitaries from North and South became a common sight on the siding. Even a president of the United States visited his friends at Maitland.

These wealthy homes, glittering carriages behind blooded horses and occupied by well-dressed folk, presented a curious spectacle in the swampy forests so dense that they are dark at high noon. The terrain swarmed with the deadly diamondback rattlesnake, and huge, decades-old bull alligators bellowed their challenge from the uninhabited shores of lakes. It was necessary to carry a lantern when one walked out at night, to avoid stumbling over these immense reptiles in the streets of Maitland.

Roads were made by the simple expedient of driving buggies and wagons back and forth over the foot trail, which ran for seven miles between Maitland and Orlando. The terrain was as flat as a table and totally devoid of rocks. All the roadmakers had to do was to curve around the numerous big pine trees and oaks. It seems it was too much trouble to cut them down. Therefore, the road looked as if it had been laid out by a playful snake. Now and then somebody would chop down a troublesome tree. Way late, the number of tree stumps along the route began to be annoying. Buggy wheels bumped and jolted over them and took away the pleasure of driving. So a man was hired to improve the road. His instructions were to round off the tops of all stumps so that the wheels, if and when they struck stumps, would slide off gently instead of jolting the teeth out of riders as before. This was done, and the spanking rigs of the bloods whisked along with more assurance.

Now, the Negro population of Maitland settled simultaneously with the white. They had been needed, and found profitable employment. The best of relations existed between employer and employee. While the white estates flourished on the three-mile length of Lake Maitland, the Negroes set up their hastily built shacks around St. John's Hole, a lake as round as a dollar, and less than a half-mile wide. It is now a beauty spot in the heart of Maitland, hard by United States Highway Number 17. They call it Lake Lily.

The Negro women could be seen every day but Sunday squatting around St. John's Hole on their haunches, primitive style, washing clothes and fishing, while their men went forth and made their support in cutting new ground, building, and planting orange groves. Things were moving so swiftly that there was plenty to do, with good pay. Other Negroes in Georgia and West Florida heard of the boom in South Florida from Crescent City to Cocoa and they came. No more back-bending over rows of cotton; no more fear of the fury of the Reconstruction. Good pay, sympathetic white folks and cheap land, soft to the touch of a plow. Relatives and friends were sent for.

Two years after the three adventurers entered the primeval forests of Mosquito County, Maitland had grown big enough, and simmered down enough, to consider a formal city government.

Now, these founders were, to a man, people who had risked their lives and fortunes that Negroes might be free. Those who had fought in the ranks had thrown their weight behind the cause of Emancipation. So when it was decided to hold an election, the Eatons, Lawrences, Vanderpools, Hurds, Halls, the Hills, Yateses and Galloways, and all the rest including Bishop Whipple, head of the

Minnesota diocese, never for a moment considered excluding the Negroes from participation. The whites nominated a candidate, and the Negroes, under the aggressive lead of Joe Clarke, a muscular, dynamic Georgia Negro, put up Tony Taylor as their standard-bearer.

I do not know whether it was the numerical superiority of the Negroes, or whether some of the whites, out of deep feeling, threw their votes to the Negro side. At any rate, Tony Taylor became the first mayor of Maitland with Joe Clarke winning out as town marshal. This was a wholly unexpected turn, but nobody voiced any open objections. The Negro mayor and marshal and the white city council took office peacefully and served their year without incident.

But during that year, a yeast was working. Joe Clarke had asked himself, why not a Negro town? Few of the Negroes were interested. It was too vaulting for their comprehension. A pure Negro town! If nothing but their own kind was in it, who was going to run it? With no white folks to command them, how would they know what to do? Joe Clarke had plenty of confidence in himself to do the job, but few others could conceive of it.

But one day by chance or purpose, Joe Clarke was telling of his ambitions to Captain Eaton, who thought it a workable plan. He talked it over with Captain Lawrence and others. By the end of the year, all arrangements had been made. Lawrence and Eaton bought a tract of land a mile west of Maitland for a town site. The backing of the whites helped Joe Clarke to convince the other Negroes, and things were settled.

Captain Lawrence at his own expense erected a well-built

church on the new site, and Captain Eaton built a hall for general assembly and presented it to the new settlement. A little later, the wife of Bishop Whipple had the first church rolled across the street and built a larger church on the same spot, and the first building was to become a library, stocked with books donated by the white community.

So on August 18, 1886, the Negro town, called Eatonville, after Captain Eaton, received its charter of incorporation from the state capital, Tallahassee, and made history by becoming the first of its kind in America, and perhaps in the world. So, in a raw, bustling frontier, the experiment of self-government for Negroes was tried. White Maitland and Negro Eatonville have lived side by side for fifty-six years without a single instance of enmity. The spirit of the founders has reached beyond the grave.

The whole lake country of Florida sprouted with life—mostly Northerners, and prosperity was everywhere. It was in the late eighties that the stars fell, and many of the original settlers date their coming "just before, or just after the stars fell."

INTO THIS BURLY, boiling, hard-hitting, rugged-individualistic setting walked one day a tall, heavy-muscled mulatto who resolved to put down roots.

John Hurston, in his late twenties, had left Macon County, Alabama, because the ordeal of share-cropping on a southern Alabama cotton plantation was crushing to his ambition. There was no rise to the thing.

He had been born near Notasulga, Alabama, in an outlying

district of landless Negroes, and whites not too much better off. It was "over the creek," which was just like saying on the wrong side of the railroad tracks. John Hurston had learned to read and write somehow between cotton-choppings and cotton-picking, and it might have satisfied him in a way. But somehow he took to going to Macedonia Baptist Church on the right side of the creek. He went one time, and met up with dark-brown Lucy Ann Potts, of the land-owning Richard Potts, which might have given him the going habit.

He was nearly twenty years old then, and she was fourteen. My mother used to claim with a smile that she saw him looking and looking at her up there in the choir and wondered what he was looking for. She wasn't studying about *him*. However, when the service was over and he kept standing around, never far from her, she asked somebody, "Who is dat bee-stung yaller nigger?"

"Oh, dat's one of dem niggers from over de creek, one of dem Hurstons—call him John I believe."

That was supposed to settle that. Over-the-creek niggers lived from one white man's plantation to the other. Regular hand-to-mouth folks. Didn't own pots to pee in, nor beds to push 'em under. Didn't have no more pride than to let themselves be hired by poor-white trash. No more to 'em than the stuffings out of a zero. The inference was that Lucy Ann Potts had asked about nothing and had been told.

Mama thought no more about him, she said. Of course, she couldn't help noticing that his gray-green eyes and light skin stood out sharply from the black-skinned, black-eyed crowd he was in.

Then, too, he had a build on him that made you look. A stud-looking buck like that would have brought a big price in slavery time. Then, if he had not kept on hanging around where she couldn't help from seeing him, she would never have remembered that she had seen him two or three times before around the cotton-gin in Notasulga, and once in a store. She had wondered then who he was, handling bales of cotton like suitcases.

After that Sunday, he got right worrisome. Slipping her notes between the leaves of hymn-books and things like that. It got so bad that a few months later she made up her mind to marry him just to get rid of him. So she did, in spite of the most violent opposition of her family. She put on the little silk dress which she had made with her own hands, out of goods bought from egg-money she had saved. Her ninety pounds of fortitude set out on her wedding night alone, since none of the family except her brother Jim could bear the sight of her great come-down in the world. She who was considered the prettiest and the smartest black girl was throwing herself away and disgracing the Pottses by marrying an over-the-creek nigger, and a bastard at that. Folks said he was a certain white man's son. But here she was, setting out to walk two miles at night by herself, to keep her pledge to him at the church. Her father, more tolerant than her mother, decided that his daughter was not going alone, nor was she going to walk to her wedding. So he hitched up the buggy and went with her. Nobody much was there. Her brother Jim slipped in just before she stood on the floor.

So she said her words and took her stand for life, and went

off to a cabin on a plantation with him. She never forgot how the late moon shone that night as his two hundred pounds of bone and muscle shoved open the door and lifted her in his arms over the doorsill.

That cabin on a white man's plantation had to be all for the present. She had been pointedly made to know that the Potts plantation was nothing to her any more. Her father soon softened and was satisfied to an extent, but her mother, never. To her dying day her daughter's husband was never John Hurston to her. He was always "Dat yaller bastard." Four years after my mother's marriage, and during her third pregnancy, she got to thinking of the five acres of clingstone peaches on her father's place, and the yearning was so strong that she walked three miles to get a few. She was holding the corners of her apron with one hand and picking peaches with the other when her mother spied her, and ordered her off the place.

It was after his marriage that my father began to want things. Plantation life began to irk and bind him. His over-the-creek existence was finished. What else was there for a man like him? He left his wife and three children behind and went out to seek and see.

Months later he pitched into the hurly-burly of South Florida. So he heard about folks building a town all out of colored people. It seemed like a good place to go. Later on, he was to be elected Mayor of Eatonville for three terms, and to write the local laws. The village of Eatonville is still governed by the laws formulated by my father. The town clerk still consults a copy of the original printing which seems to be the only one in existence now. I have tried every way I know how to get this copy for my library, but so far it has not been possible. I had it once, but the town clerk came and took it back.

When my mother joined Papa a year after he had settled in Eatonville, she brought some quilts, her featherbed and bedstead. That was all they had in the house that night. Two burlap bags were stuffed with Spanish moss for the two older children to sleep on. The youngest child was taken into the bed with them.

So these two began their new life. Both of them swore that things were going to better, and it came to pass as they said. They bought land, built a roomy house, planted their acres and reaped. Children kept coming—more mouths to feed and more feet for shoes. But neither of them seemed to have minded that. In fact, my father not only boasted among other men about "his house full of young'uns" but he boasted that he had never allowed his wife to go out and hit a lick of work for anybody a day in her life. Of weakness, he had his share, and I know that my mother was very unhappy at times, but neither of them ever made any move to call the thing off. In fact, on two occasions, I heard my father threaten to kill my mother if she ever started towards the gate to leave him. He was outraged and angry one day when she said lightly that if he did not want to do for her and his children, there was another man over the fence waiting for his job. That expression is a folk-saying and Papa had heard it used hundreds of times by other women, but he was outraged at hearing it from Mama. She definitely understood, before he got through carrying on, that the saying was not for her lips.

On another occasion Papa got the idea of escorting the wife of one of his best friends, and having the friend escort Mama. But

Mama seemed to enjoy it more than Papa thought she ought to—though she had opposed the idea when it was suggested—and it ended up with Papa leaving his friend's wife at the reception and following Mama and his friend home, and marching her into the house with the muzzle of his Winchester rifle in her back. The friend's wife, left alone at the hall, gave both her husband and Papa a good cussing out the next day. Mama dared not laugh, even at that, for fear of stirring Papa up more. It was a month or so before the two families thawed out again. Even after that, the subject could never be mentioned before Papa or the friend's wife, though both of them had been red-hot for the experiment.

My mother rode herd on one woman with a horsewhip about Papa, and "spoke out" another one. This, instead of making Papa angry, seemed to please him ever so much. The woman who got "spoken out" threatened to whip my mother. Mama was very small and the other woman was husky. But when Papa heard of the threats against Mama, he notified the outside woman that if she could not whip him too, she had better not bring the mess up. The woman left the county without ever breaking another breath with Papa. Nobody around there knew what became of her.

So, looking back, I take it that Papa and Mama, in spite of his meanderings, were really in love. Maybe he was just born before his time.

WE LIVED ON a big piece of ground with two big chinaberry trees shading the front gate and Cape jasmine bushes with hundreds of blooms on either side of the walks. I loved the fleshy, white, fragrant blooms as a child but did not make too much of them. They were too common in my neighborhood. When I got to New York and found out that the people called them gardenias, and that the flowers cost a dollar each, I was impressed. The home folks laughed when I went back down there and told them. Some of the folks did not want to believe me. A dollar for a Cape jasmine bloom! Folks up north there must be crazy.

There were plenty of orange, grapefruit, tangerine, guavas and other fruits in our yard. We had a five-acre garden with things to eat growing in it, and so we were never hungry. We had chicken on the table often; home-cured meat, and all the eggs we wanted. It was a common thing for us smaller children to fill the iron tea-kettle full of eggs and boil them, and lay around in the yard and eat them until we were full. Any left-over boiled eggs could always be used for missiles. There was plenty of fish in the lakes around the town, and so we had all that we wanted. But beef stew was something rare. We were all very happy whenever Papa went to Orlando and brought back something delicious like stew-beef. Chicken and fish were too common with us. In the same way, we treasured an apple. We had oranges, tangerines and grapefruit to use as hand-grenades on the neighbors' children. But apples were something rare. They came from way up north.

Our house had eight rooms, and we called it a two-story house; but later on I learned it was really one story and a jump. The big boys all slept up there, and it was a good place to hide and shirk from sweeping off the front porch or raking up the back yard.

Downstairs in the dining-room there was an old "safe," a punched design in its tin doors. Glasses of guava jelly, quart jars of pear, peach and other kinds of preserves. The left-over cooked foods were on the lower shelves.

There were eight children in the family, and our house was noisy from the time school turned out until bedtime. After supper we gathered in Mama's room, and everybody had to get their lessons for the next day. Mama carried us all past long division in arithmetic, and parsing sentences in grammar, by diagrams on the blackboard. That was as far as she had gone. Then the younger ones were turned over to my oldest brother, Bob, and Mama sat and saw to it that we paid attention. You had to keep on going over things until you did know. How I hated the multiplication tables—especially the sevens!

We had a big barn, and a stretch of ground well covered with Bermuda grass. So on moonlight nights, two-thirds of the village children from seven to eighteen would be playing hide and whoop, chick-mah-chick, hide and seek, and other boisterous games in our yard. Once or twice a year we might get permission to go and play at some other house. But that was most unusual. Mama contended that we had plenty of space to play in; plenty of things to play with; and, furthermore, plenty of us to keep each other's company. If she had her way, she meant to raise her children to stay at home. She said that there was no need for us to live like no-count Negroes and poor-white trash—too poor to sit in the house—had to come outdoors for any pleasure, or hang around somebody else's house. Any of her children who had any tendencies like that must have got it from the Hurston side. It certainly did not come from the Pottses. Things like that gave me my first glimmering of the universal female gospel that all good traits and leanings come from the mother's side.

Mama exhorted her children at every opportunity to "jump at de sun." We might not land on the sun, but at least we would get off the ground. Papa did not feel so hopeful. Let well enough alone. It did not do for Negroes to have too much spirit. He was always threatening to break mine or kill me in the attempt. My mother was always standing between us. She conceded that I was impudent and given to talking back, but she didn't want to "squinch my spirit" too much for fear that I would turn out to be a mealy-mouthed rag doll by the time I got grown. Papa always flew hot when Mama said that. I do not know whether he feared for my future, with the tendency I had to stand and give battle, or that he felt a personal reference in Mama's observation. He predicted dire things for me. The white folks were not going to stand for it. I was going to be hung before I got grown. Somebody was going to blow me down for my sassy tongue. Mama was going to suck sorrow for not beating my temper out of me before it was too late. Posses with ropes and guns were going to drag me out sooner or later on account of that stiff neck I toted. I was going to tote a hungry belly by reason of my forward ways. My older sister was meek and mild. She would always get along. Why couldn't I be like her? Mama would keep right on with whatever she was doing and remark, "Zora is my young'un and Sarah is yours. I'll be bound mine will come out more than conquer. You leave her alone. I'll tend to her when I figger she needs it." She meant by that that Sarah had a disposition like Papa's, while mine was like hers.

Behind Mama's rocking-chair was a good place to be in times like that. Papa was not going to hit Mama. He was two hundred pounds of bone and muscle and Mama weighed somewhere in the nineties. When people teased him about Mama being the boss, he would say he could break her of her headstrong ways if he wanted to, but she was so little that he couldn't find any place to hit her. My Uncle Jim, Mama's brother, used to always take exception to that. He maintained that if a woman had anything big enough to sit on, she had something big enough to hit on. That was his firm conviction, and he meant to hold on to it as long as the bottom end of his backbone pointed to the ground—don't care who the woman was or what she looked like, or where she came from. Men like Papa who held to any other notion were just beating around the bush, dodging the issue, and otherwise looking like a fool at the funeral.

Papa used to shake his head at this and say, "What's de use of me taking my fist to a poor weakly thing like a women? Anyhow, you got to submit yourself to em, so there ain't no use in beating on 'em and then have to go back and beg 'em pardon."

But perhaps the real reason that Papa did not take Uncle Jim's advice too seriously was because he saw how it worked out in Uncle Jim's own house. He could tackle Aunt Caroline, all right, but he had his hands full to really beat her. A knockdown didn't convince her that the fight was over at all. She would get up and come right on in, and she was nobody's weakling. It was generally conceded that he might get the edge on her in physical combat if he took a hammer or a trace-chain to her, but in other ways she always won. She would watch his various philandering episodes just so long, and then she would go into action. One time she saw all, and said nothing. But one Saturday afternoon, she watched him rush in with a new shoe-box which he thought that she did not see him take out to the barn and hide until he was ready to go out. Just as the sun went down, he went out, got his box, cut across the orange grove and went on down to the store.

He stopped long enough there to buy a quart of peanuts, two stalks of sugarcane, and then tripped on off to the little house in the woods where lived a certain transient light of love. Aunt Caroline kept right on ironing until he had gotten as far as the store. Then she slipped on her shoes, went out in the yard and got the axe, slung it across her shoulder and went walking very slowly behind him.

The men on the store porch had given Uncle Jim a laughing sendoff. They all knew where he was going and why. The shoes had been bought right there at the store. Now here came "dat Cal'line" with her axe on her shoulder. No chance to warn Uncle Jim at all. Nobody expected murder, but they knew that plenty of trouble was on the way. So they just sat and waited. Cal'line had done so many side-splitting things to Jim's lights of love—all without a single comment from her—that they were on pins to see what happened next.

About an hour later, when it was almost black dark, they saw a furtive figure in white dodging from tree to tree until it hopped over Clark's strawberry-patch fence and headed towards

Uncle Jim's house until it disappeared.

"Looked mightily like a man in long drawers and nothing else," Walter Thomas observed. Everybody agreed that it did, but who and what could it be?

By the time the town lamp which stood in front of the store was lighted, Aunt Caroline emerged from the blackness that hid the woods and passed the store. The axe was still over her shoulder, but now it was draped with Uncle Jim's pants, shirt and coat. A new pair of women's oxfords were dangling from the handle by their strings. Two stalks of sugarcane were over her other shoulder. All she said was, "Good evening, gentlemen," and kept right on walking towards home.

The porch rocked with laughter. They had the answer to everything. Later on when they asked Uncle Jim how Cal'line managed to get into the lady's house, he smiled sourly and said, "Dat axe was her key." When they kept on teasing him, he said, "Oh dat old stubborn woman I married, you can't teach her nothing. I can't teach her no city ways at all."

On another occasion, she caused another lady who couldn't give the community anything but love, baby, to fall off of the high, steep church steps on her head. Aunt Cal'line might have done that just to satisfy her curiosity, since it was said that the lady felt that anything more than a petticoat under her dresses would be an encumbrance. Maybe Aunt Caroline just wanted to verify the rumor. The way the lady tumbled, it left no doubt in the matter. She was really a free soul. Evidently Aunt Caroline was put out about it, because she had to expectorate at that very moment, and it just happened to land where the lady was bare. Aunt Caroline evidently tried to correct her error in spitting on her rival, for she took her foot and tried to grind it in. She never said a word as usual, so the lady must have misunderstood Aunt Caroline's curiosity. She left town in a hurry—a speedy hurry—and never was seen in those parts again.

So Papa did not take Uncle Jim's philosophy about handling the lady people too seriously. Every time Mama cornered him about some of his doings, he used to threaten to wring a chair over her head. She never even took enough notice of the threat to answer. She just went right on asking questions about his doings and then answering them herself until Papa slammed out of the house looking like he had been whipped all over with peach hickories. But I had better not let out a giggle at such times, or it would be just too bad.

Our house was a place where people came. Visiting preachers, Sunday school and B.Y.P.U. workers, and just friends. There was fried chicken for visitors, and other such hospitality as the house afforded.

Papa's bedroom was the guest-room. Store-bought towels would be taken out of the old round-topped trunk in Mama's room and draped on the washstand. The pitcher and bowl were scrubbed out before fresh water from the pump was put in for the use of the guest. Sweet soap was company soap. We knew that. Otherwise, Octagon laundry soap was used to keep us clean. Bleached-out meal sacks served the family for bath towels ordinarily, so that the store-bought towels could be nice and clean for visitors.

Company got the preference in toilet paper, too. Old newspapers were put out in the privy house for family use. But when company came, something better was offered them. Fair to middling guests got sheets out of the old Sears, Roebuck catalogue. But Mama would sort over her old dress patterns when really fine company came, and the privy house was well scrubbed, lime thrown in, and the soft tissue paper pattern stuck on a nail inside the place for the comfort and pleasure of our guests.

Tennessee Williams

THE DIVING BELL

I WANT TO go under the sea in a diving-bell

and return to the surface with ominous wonders to tell.

I want to be able to say:

"The base is unstable, it's probably unable

to weather much weather,

being all hung together by a couple of blond hairs caught

in a fine-toothed comb."

I want to be able to say through a P.A. system,

authority giving a sonorous tone to the vowels,

"I'm speaking from Neptune's bowels.

The sea's floor is nacreous, filmy

Tennessee Williams's haunting plays include A Streetcar Named Desire, Cat on a Hot Tin Roof, *and* Suddenly, Last Summer. *This unusual poem is set in Key West, where he moved in 1941, because, as he put it, "I like to swim."*

with milk in the wind, the light of an overcast morning."

I want to give warning:
      "The pediment of our land is a lady's comb,
      the basement is moored to the dome
by a pair of blond hairs caught in a delicate
tortoise-shell comb."

I think it is safer to roam
      than to stay in a mortgaged home
         And so—

I want to go under the sea in a bubble of glass
containing a sofa upholstered in green corduroy
and a girl for practical purposes and a boy
      well-versed in the classics.

I want to be first to go down there where action is slow
      but thought is surprisingly quick.
      It's only a dare-devil's trick,
      the length of a burning wick
      between tu-whit and tu-who!

      Oh, it's pretty and blue
but not at all to be trusted. No matter how deep you go
there's not very much below

the deceptive shimmer and glow

which is all for show

of sunken galleons encrusted with barnacles and doubloons,

an undersea tango palace with instant come and

go moons . . .

Cabeza de Vaca

THE COUNTRY WHERE we came on shore to this town and region of Apalachen is for the most part level, the ground of sand and stiff earth. Throughout are immense trees and open woods, in which are walnut, laurel, and another tree called liquid-amber,[1] cedars, savins, evergreen oaks, pines, red-oaks, and palmitos like those of Spain. There are many lakes, great and small, over every part of it; some troublesome of fording, on account of depth and the great number of trees lying throughout them. Their beds are sand. The lakes in the country of Apalachen are much larger than those we found before coming there.[2]

In this province are many maize fields; and the houses are

Cabeza de Vaca was the first Spanish explorer to reach the United States, landing in the swampy lake country of north Florida. This excerpt is from his 1528 journal. Note the description of an opossum in the second paragraph, the first printed reference to this beast.

scattered as are those of the Gelves. There are deer of three kinds, rabbits, hares, bears, lions, and other wild beasts. Among them we saw an animal with a pocket on its belly,[3] in which it carries its young until they know how to seek food, and if it happen that they should be out feeding and any one come near, the mother will not run until she has gathered them in together. The country is very cold.[4] It has fine pastures for herds. Birds are of various kinds. Geese in great numbers. Ducks, mallards, royal-ducks, fly-catchers, night-herons and partridges abound. We saw many falcons, gerfalcons, sparrow-hawks, merlins, and numerous other fowl.[5]

Two hours after our arrival at Apalachen, the Indians who had fled from there came in peace to us, asking for their women and children, whom we released; but the detention of a cacique by the Governor produced great excitement, in consequence of which they returned for battle early the next day, and attacked us with such promptness and alacrity that they succeeded in setting fire to the houses in which we were. As we sallied they fled to the lakes near by, because of which and the large maize fields we could do them no injury, save in the single instance of one Indian, whom we killed. The day following, others came against us from a town on the opposite side of the lake, and attacked us as the first had done, escaping in the same way, except one who was also slain.

We were in the town twenty-five days, in which time we made three incursions, and found the country very thinly peopled and difficult to travel for the bad passages, the woods and lakes. We inquired of the cacique we kept and the natives we brought with us, who were the neighbors and enemies of these Indians, as to the nature of the country, the character and condition of the inhabitants, of the food and all other matters concerning it. Each answered apart from the rest, that the largest town in all that region was Apalachen; the people beyond were less numerous and poorer, the land little occupied, and the inhabitants much scattered; that thenceforward were great lakes, dense forests, immense deserts and solitudes. We then asked touching the region towards the south, as to the towns and subsistence in it. They said that in keeping such a direction, journeying nine days, there was a town called Aute,[6] the inhabitants whereof had much maize, beans, and pumpkins, and being near the sea they had fish, and that those people were their friends.

In view of the poverty of the land, the unfavorable accounts of the population and of everything else we heard, the Indians making continual war upon us, wounding our people and horses at the places where they went to drink, shooting from the lakes with such safety to themselves that we could not retaliate, killing a lord of Tescuco, named Don Pedro,[7] whom the commissary brought with him, we determined to leave that place and go in quest of the sea, and the town of Aute of which we were told.

At the termination of the twenty-five days[8] after our arrival we departed,[9] and on the first day got through those lakes and passages without seeing any one, and on the second day we came to a lake difficult of crossing, the water reaching to the paps, and in it were numerous logs. On reaching the middle of it we were attacked by many Indians from behind trees, who thus covered themselves that we might not get sight of them, and others were on the fallen tim-bers. They drove their arrows with such effect that they wounded many men and horses, and before we got through the lake they took our guide. They now followed, endeavoring to contest our passage; but our coming out afforded no relief, nor gave us any better position; for when we wished to fight them they retired immediately into the lake, whence they continued to wound our men and beasts. The Governor, seeing this, commanded the cavalry to dismount and charge the Indians on foot. Accordingly the comptroller[10] alighting with the rest, attacked them, when they all turned and ran into the lake at hand, and thus the passage was gained.

Some of our men were wounded in this conflict, for whom the good armor they wore did not avail. There were those this day who swore that they had seen two red oaks, each the thickness of the lower part of the leg, pierced through from side to side by arrows; and this is not so much to be wondered at, considering the power and skill with which the Indians are able to project them. I myself saw an arrow that had entered the butt of an elm to the depth of a span.

The Indians we had so far seen in Florida are all archers. They go naked, are large of body, and appear at a distance like giants. They are of admirable proportions, very spare and of great activity and strength. The bows they use are as thick as the arm, of eleven or twelve palms in length, which they will discharge at two hundred paces with so great precision that they miss nothing.

Having got through this passage, at the end of a league we arrived at another of the same character, but worse, as it was longer,

being half a league in extent. This we crossed freely, without inter-
ruption from the Indians, who, as they had spent on the former occasion their store of arrows, had nought with which they dared venture
to engage us. Going through a similar passage the next day, I discovered the trail of persons ahead, of which I gave notice to the
Governor, who was in the rear-guard, so that though the Indians
came upon us, as we were prepared they did no harm. After emerging
upon the plain they followed us, and we went back on them in two
directions. Two we killed, and they wounded me and two or three
others. Coming to woods we could do them no more injury, nor make
them further trouble.

In this manner we travelled eight days. After that occurrence
we were not again beset until within a league of the place to which I
have said we were going. There, while on our way, the Indians came
about us without our suspicion, and fell upon the rear-guard. A hidalgo,
named Avellaneda, hearing the cries of his serving boy, went back to
give assistance, when he was struck by an arrow near the edge of his
cuirass; and so severe was the wound, the shaft having passed almost
entirely through his neck, that he presently died. The corpse was carried to Aute, where we arrived at the end of nine days'[11] travel from
Apalache. We found all the inhabitants gone and the houses burned.
Maize, beans, and pumpkins were in great plenty, all beginning to be
fit for gathering. Having rested two days, the Governor begged me to
go and look for the sea, as the Indians said it was near; and we had
before discovered it, while on the way, from a very large stream, to
which we had given the name of River of the Magdalena.[12]

Accordingly, I set out the next day after, in company with the commissary, Captain Castillo, Andrés Dorantes, seven more on horseback, and fifty on foot. We travelled until the hour of vespers, when we arrived at a road or entrance of the sea. Oysters were abundant, over which the men rejoiced, and we gave thanks to God that he had brought us there. The following morning[13] I sent twenty men to explore the coast and ascertain its direction. They returned the night after, reporting that those creeks and bays were large, and lay so far inland as made it difficult to examine them agreeably to our desires, and that the sea shore was very distant.

These tidings obtained, seeing our slender means, and condition for exploring the coast, I went back to the Governor. On our arrival we found him and many others sick. The Indians had assaulted them the night before, and because of the malady that had come upon them, they had been pushed to extremity. One of the horses had been killed. I gave a report of what I had done, and of the embarrassing nature of the country. We remained there that day.

THE NEXT MORNING[14] we left Aute, and travelled all day before coming to the place I had visited. The journey was extremely arduous. There were not horses enough to carry the sick, who went on increasing in numbers day by day, and we knew of no cure. It was piteous and painful to witness our perplexity and distress. We saw on our arrival how small were the means for advancing farther. There was not anywhere to go; and if there had been, the people were unable to move forward, the greater part being ill, and those were few who could be on duty. I cease here to relate more of this, because any one may suppose what would occur in a country so remote and malign, so destitute of all resource, whereby either to live in it or go out of it; but most certain assistance is in God, our Lord, on whom we never failed to place reliance. One thing occurred, more afflicting to us than all the rest, which was, that of the persons mounted, the greater part commenced secretly to plot, hoping to secure a better fate for themselves by abandoning the Governor and the sick, who were in a state of weakness and prostration. But, as among them were many hidalgos and persons of gentle condition, they would not permit this to go on, without informing the Governor and the officers of your Majesty; and as we showed them the deformity of their purpose, and placed before them the moment when they should desert their captain, and those who were ill and feeble, and above all the disobedience to the orders of your Majesty, they determined to remain, and that whatever might happen to one should be the lot of all, without any forsaking the rest.

After the accomplishment of this, the Governor called them all to him, and of each apart he asked advice as to what he should do to get out of a country so miserable, and seek that assistance else-where which could not here be found, a third part of the people being very sick, and the number increasing every hour; for we regarded it as certain that we should all become so, and could pass out of it only through death, which from its coming in such a place was to us all the more terrible. These, with many other embarrass-ments being considered, and entertaining many plans, we coincided in one great project extremely difficult to put in operation, and that was to build vessels in which we might go away. This appeared impossible to every one; we knew not how to construct, nor were there tools, nor iron, nor forge, nor tow, nor resin, nor rigging; finally, no one thing of so many that are necessary, nor any man who had a knowledge of their manufacture; and, above all, there was nothing to eat, while building, for those who should labor. Reflecting on all this, we agreed to think of the subject with more deliberation, and the conversation dropped from that day, each going his way, commending our course to God, our Lord, that he would direct it as should best serve Him.

The next day it was His will that one of the company should come saying that he could make some pipes out of wood, which with deer-skins might be made into bellows; and, as we lived in a time when anything that had the semblance of relief appeared well, we told him to set himself to work. We assented to the making of nails, saws, axes, and other tools of which there was such need, from the stirrups, spurs, crossbows, and the other things of iron there were; and we laid out for support, while the work was going on, that we would make four entries into Aute, with all the horses and men that were able to go, and that on every third day a horse should be killed to be divided among those who labored in the work of the boats and the sick. The incursions were made with the people and horses that were available, and in them were brought back as many as four hundred fanegas[15] of maize; but these were not got without quarrels and contentions with the Indians. We caused many palmitos to be collected for the woof or covering, twisting and preparing it for use in the place of tow for the boats.

We commenced to build on the fourth, with the only carpenter in the company, and we proceeded with so great diligence that on the twentieth day of September five boats were finished, twenty-two cubits in length, each caulked with the fibre of the palmito. We pitched them with a certain resin, made from pine trees by a Greek, named Don Theodoro; from the same husk of the palmito, and from the tails and manes of the horses we made ropes and rigging, from our shirts, sails, and from the savins growing there we made the oars that appeared to us requisite. Such was the country into which our sins had cast us, that only by very great search could we find stone for ballast and anchors, since in it all we had not seen one. We flayed the horses, taking the skin from their legs entire, and tanning them to make bottles wherein to carry water.

During this time some went gathering shell-fish in the coves and creeks of the sea, at which employment the Indians twice attacked them and killed ten men in sight of the camp, without our being able to afford succor. We found their corpses traversed from side to side with arrows; and for all some had on good armor, it did not give adequate protection or security against the nice and powerful archery of which I have spoken. According to the declaration of our pilots under oath, from the entrance to which we had given the name Bahía de la Cruz[16] to this place, we had travelled two hundred and eighty leagues[17] or thereabout. Over all that region we had not seen a single mountain, and had no information of any whatsoever.

Before we embarked there died more than forty men of disease and hunger, without enumerating those destroyed by the Indians. By the twenty-second of the month of September, the horses had been consumed, one only remaining; and on that day we embarked in the following order: In the boat of the Governor went forty-nine men; in another, which he gave to the comptroller and the commissary, went as many others; the third, he gave to Captain Alonzo del Castillo and Andrés Dorantes, with forty-eight men; and another he gave to two captains, Tellez and Peñalosa, with forty-seven men. The last was given to the assessor and myself, with forty-nine men. After the provisions and clothes had been taken in, not over a span of the gunwales remained above water; and more than this, the boats were so crowded that we could not move: so much can necessity do, which drove us to hazard our lives in this manner, running into a turbulent sea, not a single one who went having a knowledge of navigation.[18]

THE HAVEN WE left bears the name of Bahía de Caballos.[19] We passed waist deep in water through sounds without seeing any sign of the coast, and at the close of the seventh day, we came to an island near the main. My boat went first, and from her we saw Indians approaching in five canoes, which they abandoned and left in our hands, finding that we were coming after them. The other boats passed ahead, and stopped at some houses on the island, where we found many dried mullet and roes, which were a great relief in our distress. After taking these we went on, and two leagues thence, we discovered a strait the island makes with the land,[20] which we named Sant Miguel, for having passed through it on his day.[21] Coming out we went to the coast, where with the canoes I had taken, we somewhat improved the boats, making waist-boards and securing them, so that the sides rose two palms above the water. This done we returned to move along the coast in the direction of the River Palmas,[22] our hunger and thirst continually increasing; for our scant subsistence was getting near the end, the water was out, and the bottles made from the legs of the horses having soon rotted, were useless. Sometimes we entered coves and creeks that lay far in, and found them all shallow and dangerous. Thus we journeyed along them thirty days, finding occasionally Indian fishermen, a poor and miserable lot.

At the end of this time, while the want of water was great, going near the coast at night we heard the approach of a canoe, for which, so soon as it was in sight, we paused; but it would not meet us, and, although we called, it would neither come nor wait for us. As the night was dark, we did not follow, and kept on our way. When the sun rose we saw a small island, and went to it to find water; but our labor was vain, as it had none. Lying there at anchor, a heavy storm came on, that detained us six days, we not daring to go to sea; and as it was now five days since we had drunk, our thirst was so excessive that it put us to the extremity of swallowing salt water, by which some of the men became so crazed that three or four suddenly died. I state this so briefly, because I do not believe there is any necessity for particularly relating the sufferings and toils amidst which we found ourselves; since, considering the place where we were, and the little hope we had of relief, every one may conceive much of what must have passed.

Although the storm had not ceased, as our thirst increased and the water killed us, we resolved to commend ourselves to God our Lord, and adventure the peril of the sea rather than await the end which thirst made certain. Accordingly we went out by the way we had observed the canoe go the night we came. On this day we were ourselves many times overwhelmed by the waves, and in such jeopardy that there was not one who did not suppose his death inevitable. Thanks be to Him, that in the greatest dangers, He was wont to show us his favor; for at sunset doubling a point made by the land, we found shelter with much calm.[23]

Many canoes came off with Indians who spoke with us and returned, not being disposed to await our arrival. They were of large stature and well formed: they had no bows and arrows. We followed them to their houses near by, at the edge of the water, and jumped on shore. Before their dwellings were many clay pitchers with water, and a large quantity of cooked fish, which the chief of these territories offered to the Governor and then took him to his house. Their dwellings were made of mats, and so far as we observed, were not movable. On entering the house the cacique gave us fish, and we gave him of the maize we brought, which the people ate in our presence. They asked for more and received it, and the Governor presented the cacique with many trinkets. While in the house with him, at the middle hour of night, the Indians fell suddenly upon us, and on those who were very sick, scattered along the shore.[24] They also beset the house in which the Governor was, and with a stone struck him in the face. Those of our comrades present seized the cacique; but his people being near liberated him, leaving in our hands a robe of civet-marten.

These skins are the best, I think, that can be found; they have a fragrance that can be equalled by amber and musk alone, and even at a distance is strongly perceptible. We saw there other skins, but none comparable to these.

Those of us around, finding the Governor wounded, put him into his boat; and we caused others of our people to betake themselves likewise to their boats, some fifty remaining to withstand the natives. They attacked us thrice that night, and with so great impetuosity, that on each occasion they made us retire more than a stone's cast. Not one among us escaped injury: I was wounded in the face. They had not many arrows, but had they been further provided, doubtless they would have done us much harm. In the last onset, the Captains Dorantes, Peñalosa, and Tellez put themselves in ambuscade with fifteen men, and fell upon the rear in such manner that the Indians desisted and fled.

The next morning[25] I broke up more than thirty canoes, which were serviceable for fuel in a north wind in which we were kept all day suffering severe cold, without daring to go to sea, because of the rough weather upon it. This having subsided, we again embarked, and navigated three days.[26] As we brought little water and the vessels were few, we were reduced to the last extremity. Following our course, we entered an estuary, and being there we saw Indians approaching in a canoe. We called to them and they came.

The Governor, at whose boat they first arrived, asked for water, which they assented to give, asking for something in which they might bring it, when Dorotheo Theodoro, a Greek spoken of before, said that he wished to go with them. The Governor tried to dissuade him, and so did others, but were unable; he was determined to go whatever might betide. Accordingly he went, taking with him a negro, the natives leaving two of their number as hostages. At night the Indians returned with the vessels empty and without the Christians; and when those we held were spoken to by them, they tried to plunge into the sea. Being detained by the men, the Indians in the canoe thereupon fled, leaving us sorrowful and much dejected for our loss.[27]

THE MORNING HAVING come, many natives arrived in canoes who asked us for the two that had remained in the boat. The Governor replied that he would give up the hostages when they should bring the Christians they had taken. With the Indians had come five or six chiefs,[28] who appeared to us to be the most comely persons, and of more authority and condition than any we had hitherto seen, although not so large as some others of whom we have spoken. They wore the hair loose and very long, and were covered with robes of marten such as we had before taken. Some of the robes were made up after a strange fashion, with wrought ties of lion skin, making a brave show. They entreated us to go with them, and said they would give us the Christians, water, and many other things. They continued to collect about us in canoes, attempting in them to take possession of

the mouth of that entrance; in consequence, and because it was hazardous to stay near the land, we went to sea, where they remained by
us until about mid-day. As they would not deliver our people, we
would not give up theirs; so they began to hurl clubs at us and to
throw stones with slings, making threats of shooting arrows,
although we had not seen among them all more than three or four
bows. While thus engaged, the wind beginning to freshen, they left
us and went back.

We sailed that day until the middle of the afternoon, when
my boat, which was the first, discovered a point made by the land,
and against a cape opposite, passed a broad river.[29] I cast anchor near a
little island forming the point, to await the arrival of the other boats.
The Governor did not choose to come up, and entered a bay near by
in which were a great many islets. We came together there, and took
fresh water from the sea, the stream entering it in freshet.[30] To parch
some of the maize we brought with us, since we had eaten it raw for
two days, we went on an island; but finding no wood we agreed to go
to the river beyond the point, one league off. By no effort could we
get there, so violent was the current on the way, which drove us out,
while we contended and strove to gain the land. The north wind,
which came from the shore, began to blow so strongly that it forced
us to sea without our being able to overcome it. We sounded half a
league out, and found with thirty fathoms[31] we could not get bottom;
but we were unable to satisfy ourselves that the current was not the
cause of failure. Toiling in this manner to fetch the land, we navigated
three days, and at the end of this time, a little before the sun rose, we

saw smoke in several places along the shore. Attempting to reach them, we found ourselves in three fathoms of water, and in the darkness we dared not come to land; for as we had seen so many smokes, some surprise might lie in wait, and the obscurity leave us at a loss how to act. We determined therefore to stop until morning.

When day came, the boats had lost sight of each other. I found myself in thirty fathoms. Keeping my course until the hour of vespers, I observed two boats, and drawing near I found that the first I approached was that of the Governor. He asked me what I thought we should do. I told him we ought to join the boat which went in advance, and by no means to leave her; and, the three being together, we must keep on our way to where God should be pleased to lead. He answered saying that could not be done, because the boat was far to sea and he wished to reach the shore; that if I wished to follow him, I should order the persons of my boat to take the oars and work, as it was only by strength of arm that the land could be gained. He was advised to this course by a captain with him named Pantoja, who said that if he did not fetch land that day, in six days more they would not reach it, and in that time they must inevitably famish. Discovering his will I took my oar, and so did every one his, in my boat, to obey it. We rowed until near sunset; but the Governor having in his boat the healthiest of all the men, we could not by any means hold with or follow her. Seeing this, I asked him to give me a rope from his boat, that I might be enabled to keep up with him; but he answered me that he would do much, if they, as they were, should be able to reach the land that night. I said to him, that since he saw the feeble strength we had to follow him, and do what he ordered, he must tell me how he would that I should act. He answered that it was no longer a time in which one should command another; but that each should do what he thought best to save his own life; that he so intended to act; and saying this, he departed with his boat.[32]

As I could not follow him, I steered to the other boat at sea, which waited for me, and having come up, I found her to be the one commanded by the Captains Peñalosa and Tellez.

Thus we continued in company, eating a daily allowance of half a handful of raw maize, until the end of four days, when we lost sight of each other in a storm; and such was the weather that only by God's favor we did not all go down. Because of winter and its inclemency, the many days we had suffered hunger, and the heavy beating of the waves, the people began next day to despair in such a manner that when the sun sank, all who were in my boat were fallen one on another, so near to death that there were few among them in a state of sensibility. Of the whole number at this time not five men were on their feet; and when night came, only the master and myself were left, who could work the boat. Two hours after dark, he said to me that I must take charge of her as he was in such condition he believed he should die that night. So I took the paddle, and going after midnight to see if the master was alive he said to me he was rather better, and would take the charge until day. I declare in that hour I would more willingly have died than seen so many people before me in such condition. After the master took the direction of the boat, I lay down a little while; but without repose, for nothing at that time was farther from me than sleep.

Near the dawn of day, it seemed to me I heard the tumbling of the sea; for as the coast was low, it roared loudly. Surprised at this, I called to the master, who answered me that he believed we were near the land. We sounded and found ourselves in seven fathoms. He advised that we should keep to sea until sunrise; accordingly I took an oar and pulled on the land side, until we were a league distant, when we gave her stern to the sea. Near the shore a wave took us, that knocked the boat out of water the distance of the throw of a crowbar,33 and from the violence with which she struck, nearly all the people who were in her like dead, were roused to consciousness. Finding themselves near the shore, they began to move on hands and feet, crawling to land into some ravines. There we made fire, parched some of the maize we brought, and found rain water. From the warmth of the fire the people recovered their faculties, and began somewhat to exert themselves. The day on which we arrived was the sixth of November [1528].

ENDNOTES

1The sweet-gum, copalm, or alligator tree (*Liquidambar styraciflua*).

2Seemingly the lake country in the northern part of Leon and Jefferson counties, Florida. "Apalachen" town was perhaps on Miccosukee Lake.

3The opossum. This is probably the first allusion to this animal. The name is derived from the Algonquian language of Virginia, having first been recorded by Captain John Smith.

[4] As it was now late in June, this is not explicable, unless the season was an unusual one.

[5] Buckingham Smith thinks it strange that the turkey and the alligator are not particularly mentioned among the fauna of the region.

[6] Most authorities agree that this place was at or near the site of St. Marks, south-southeast of Tallahassee, although the distance seems too short for nine days' travel, as will be seen.

[7] See Buckingham Smith, *Relation of Alvar Nuñez Cabeça de Vaca*, 1871, p. 42, note 7, regarding this Aztec prince of the blood.

[8] "Twenty-six days." Oviedo, 586. The edition of 1542 (Bandelier trans., p. 30) says: "And so we left, arriving there five days after. The first day we travelled across lagunes and trails without seeing a single Indian."

[9] July 19-20, 1528.

[10] Alonzo Enriquez.

[11] "Eight or nine days." Oviedo, 587.

[12] St. Marks River, which flows into St. Marks Bay, at the head of which Aute was situated.

[13] August 1, 1528.

[14] August 3, 1528.

[15] About six hundred and forty bushels.

[16] Tampa Bay.

[17] In reality they could not have travelled much more than as many miles in a straight line from Tampa Bay.

[18] Consult Garcilasso de la Vega, *La Florida*, 78, 1723, for the finding of the relics of Narvaez by De Soto's expedition in 1539, and see the De

Soto narration of the Gentlemen of Elvas.

[19]"Bay of Horses": St. Marks Bay of Appalachee Bay.

[20]The conditions are applicable to the mouth of St. Marks Bay, the two small islands, and the strait between them and the coast.

[21]St. Michael's Day, September 29, 1528.

[22]That is, in a southwesterly direction.

[23]Pensacola Bay. The Indians were Choctaws or a closely related tribe.

[24]"Killing three men." Oviedo, p. 589.

[25]October 28, 1528.

[26]"Three or four days." Oviedo, p. 589.

[27]Biedma's Narrative (*Publication of the Hakluyt Society*, IX. 1-83, 1851) says of the De Soto expedition in 1539: "Having set out for this village [Mavila, Mauvila, Mobile], we found a large river which we supposed to be that which falls into the bay of Chuse [Pensacola Bay]; we learned that the vessels of Narvaez had arrived there in want of water, and that a Christian named Teodoro and an Indian had remained among these Indians: at the same time they showed us a dagger which had belonged to the Christian."

[28]"Three or four," according to the Letter (Oviedo, p. 589), which also gives the number of canoes as twenty.

[29]According to the Letter they travelled two days more before reaching this point of land.

[30]The Mississippi, the waters of which were now seen by white men fourteen years before the "discovery" of the stream by De Soto.

[31]The present normal depth at this distance from the delta is about sixty feet.

32 The selfishness and incompetence of Narvaez, shown throughout the narration, are here further exemplified. His life had more than once been spared through the self-sacrifice of his men, yet he now thought more of saving himself, with the aid of his hardy crew, than of lending a hand to his weakened companions.

33 *Juego de herradura,* a game played with an iron bar, often a crowbar, which is grasped at the middle and cast as far as possible.

Elizabeth Bishop

GREGORIO VALDES, SIGN PAINTER

THE FIRST PAINTING I saw by Gregorio Valdes was in the window of a barbershop on Duval Street, the main street of Key West. The shop is in a block of cheap liquor stores, shoeshine parlors and poolrooms, all under a long wooden awning shading the sidewalk. The picture leaned against a cardboard advertisement for Eagle Whiskey, among other window decorations of red-and-green crepe-paper rosettes and streamers left over from Christmas and the announcement of an operetta at the Cuban school—all covered with dust and fly spots and littered with termites' wings.

It was a view, a real View, of a straight road diminishing to a point through green fields, and a row of straight Royal Palms on

---

It was during a 1930 fishing trip that poet Elizabeth Bishop came upon Key West and decided it would be a perfect home. Bishop is the author of numerous volumes of poetry and travel books and won the Pulitzer Prize for Poetry in 1956. "Gregorio Valdes," originally written in 1939, is from her Collected Prose.

either side, so carefully painted that one could count seven trees in each row. In the middle of the road was the tiny figure of a man on a donkey, and far away on the right the white speck of a thatched Cuban cabin that seemed to have the same mysterious properties of perspective as the little dog in Rousseau's *The Cariole of M. Juniot*. The sky was blue at the top, then white, then beautiful blush pink, the pink of a hot, mosquito-filled tropical evening. As I went back and forth in front of the barbershop on my way to the restaurant, this picture charmed me, and at last I went in and bought it for three dollars. My landlady had been trained to do "oils" at the Convent.—The house was filled with copies of *The Roman Girl at the Well, Horses in a Thunderstorm*, etc. —She was disgusted and said she would paint the same picture for me, "for fifteen cents."

The barber told me I could see more Valdes pictures in the window of a little cigar factory on Duval Street, one of the few left in Key West. There were six or seven pictures: an ugly *Last Supper* in blue and yellow, a *Guardian Angel* pushing two children along a path at the edge of a cliff, a study of flowers—all copies, and also copies of local postcards. I liked one picture of a homestead in Cuba in the same green fields, with two of the favorite Royal Palms and a banana tree, a chair on the porch, a woman, a donkey, a big white flower, and a Pan-American airplane in the blue sky. A friend bought this one, and then I decided to call on Gregorio.

He lived at 1221 Duval Street, as it said on all his pictures, but he had a "studio" around the corner in a decayed, unrentable little house. There was a palette nailed to one of the posts of the verandah with *G. Valdes, Sign Painter* on it. Inside there were three rooms with holes in the floors and weeds growing up through the holes. Gregorio had covered two sections of the walls with postcards and pictures from the newspapers. One section was animals: baby animals in zoos and wild animals in Africa. The other section was mostly reproductions of Madonnas and other religious subjects from the rotogravures. In one room there was a small plaster Virgin with some half-melted yellow wax roses in a tumbler in front of her. He also had an old cot there, and a row of plants in tin cans. One of these was Sweet Basil, which I was invited to smell every time I came to call.

Gregorio was very small, thin and sickly, with a childish face and tired brown eyes—in fact, he looked a little like the *Self-Portrait* of El Greco. He spoke very little English but was so polite that if I took someone with me who spoke Spanish he would almost ignore the Spanish and always answer in English, anyway, which made explanations and even compliments very difficult. He had been born in Key West, but his wife was from Cuba, and Spanish was the household language, as it is in most Key West Cuban families.

I commissioned him to paint a large picture of the house I was living in. When I came to take him to see it he was dressed in new clothes: a new straw hat, a new striped shirt, buttoned up but without a necktie, his old trousers, but a pair of new black-and-white Cuban shoes, elaborately Gothic in design, and with such pointed toes that they must have been very uncomfortable. I gave him an enlarged photograph of the house to paint from and also asked to have more flowers put in, a monkey that lived next door, a parrot, and a certain type of palm tree, called the Traveler's Palm. There is only one of these in Key West, so Gregorio went and made a careful drawing of it to go by. He showed me the drawing later, with the measurements and colors written in along the side, and apologized because the tree really had seven branches on one side and six on the other, but in the painting he had given both sides seven to make it more symmetrical. He put in flowers in profusion, and the parrot, on the perch on the verandah, and painted the monkey, larger than life-size, climbing the trunk of the palm tree.

When he delivered this picture there was no one at home, so he left it on the verandah leaning against the wall. As I came home that evening I saw it there from a long way off down the street—a fair-sized copy of the house, in green and white, leaning against its green-and-white prototype. In the gray twilight they seemed to blur together and I had the feeling that if I came closer I would be able to see another miniature copy of the house leaning on the porch of the painted house, and so on—like the Old Dutch Cleanser advertisements. A few days later when I had hung the picture I asked Gregorio to a vernissage party, and in spite of language difficulties we all had a very nice time. We drank sherry, and from time to time Gregorio would announce, "More wine."

He had never seemed very well, but this winter when I returned to Key West he seemed much more delicate than before. After Christmas I found him at work in his studio only once. He had several commissions for pictures and was very happy. He had changed the little palette that said *Sign Painter* for a much larger one

saying *Artist Painter*. But the next time I went to see him he was at
the house on Duval Street and one of his daughters told me he was
"seek" and in bed. Gregorio came out as she said it, however, pulling
on his trousers and apologizing for not having any new pictures to
show, but he looked very ill.

His house was a real Cuban house, very bare, very clean,
with a bicycle standing in the narrow front hall. The living room
had a doorway draped with green chenille Christmas fringe, and six
straight chairs around a little table in the middle bearing a bunch of
artificial flowers. The bareness of a Cuban house, and the apparent
remoteness of every object in it from every other object, gives one
the same sensation as the bareness and remoteness of Gregorio's best
pictures. The only decorations I remember seeing in the house were
the crochet and embroidery work being done by one of the daughters, which was always on the table in the living room, and a few
photographs—of Gregorio when he had played the trombone in a
band as a young man, a wedding party, etc., and a marriage certificate, hanging on the walls. Also in the hall there was a wonderful
clock. The case was a plaster statue, painted bronze, of President
Roosevelt manipulating a ship's wheel. On the face there was a picture of a barkeeper shaking cocktails, and the little tin shaker actually
shook up and down with the ticking of the clock. I think this must
have been won at one of the bingo tents that are opened at Key
West every winter.

Gregorio grew steadily worse during the spring. His own
doctor happened to be in Cuba and he refused to have any other

come to see him. His daughters said that when they begged him to
have a doctor he told them that if one came he would "throw him
away."

A friend and I went to see him about the first of May. It was
the first time he had failed to get up to see us and we realized that he
was dangerously sick. The family took us to a little room next to the
kitchen, about six feet wide, where he lay on a low cot-bed. The
room was only large enough to hold the bed, a wardrobe, a little
stand, and a slop-jar, and the rented house was in such a bad state of
repair that light came up through the big holes in the floor. Gregorio,
terribly emaciated, lay in bed wearing a blue shirt; his head was on a
flat pillow, and just above him a little holy picture was tacked to the
wall. He looked like one of those Mexican retablo paintings of miraculous cures, only in his case we were afraid no miraculous cure was
possible.

That day we bought one of the few pictures he had on
hand—a still life of Key West fruits such as a coconut, a mango,
sapodillos, a watermelon, and a sugar apple, all stiffly arranged against
a blue background. In this picture the paint had cracked slightly, and
examining it I discovered one eccentricity of Gregorio's painting. The
blue background extended all the way to the tabletop and where the
paint had cracked the blue showed through the fruit. Apparently he
had felt that since the wall was back of the fruit he should paint it
there, before he could go on and paint the fruit in front of it.

The next day we discovered in the Sunday *New York Times*
that he had a group of fifteen paintings on exhibition at the Artists'

Gallery in New York. We cut out the notice and took it to his house, but he was so sick he could only lie in bed holding out his thin arms and saying "Excuse, excuse." We were relieved, however, when the family told us that he had at last consented to have another doctor come to see him.

On the evening of the ninth of May we were extremely shocked when a Cuban friend we met on the street told us that "Gregorio died at five o'clock." We drove to the house right away. Several people were standing on the verandah in the dark, talking in low voices. One young man came up and said to us, "The old man die at five o'clock." He did not mean to be disrespectful but his English was poor and he said "old man" instead of "father."

The funeral took place the next afternoon. Only relatives and close friends attend the service of a Cuban funeral and only men go to the cemetery, so there were a great many cars drawn up in front of the house filled with the waiting men. Very quickly the coffin was carried out, covered with the pale, loose Rock Roses that the Valdeses grow for sale in their back yard. Afterwards we were invited in, "to see the children."

Gregorio was so small and had such a detached manner that it was always surprising to think of him as a patriarch. He had five daughters and two sons: Jennie, Gregorio, Florencio, Anna Louisa, Carmela, Adela, and Estella. Two of the daughters are married and he had three grandchildren, two boys and a girl.

I had been afraid that when I brought him the clipping from the *Times* he had been too sick to understand it, but the youngest daughter told me that he had looked at it a great deal and had kept telling them all that he was "going to get the first prize for painting in New York."

She told me several other anecdotes about her father—how when the battleships came into Key West harbor during the war he had made a large-scale model of one of them, exact in every detail, and had used it as an ice-cream cart, to peddle Cuban ices through the streets. It attracted the attention of a tourist from the North and he bought it, "for eighty dollars." She said that when the carnivals came to town he would sit up all night by the light of an oil lamp, making little pinwheels to sell. He used to spend many nights at his studio, too, when he wanted to finish a sign or a picture, getting a little sleep on the cot there.

He had learned to paint when he and his wife were "sweethearts," she said, from an old man they call a name that sounds like "Musi"—no one knows how to spell it or remembers his real name. This old man lived in a house belonging to the Valdeses, but he was too poor to pay rent and so he gave Gregorio painting lessons instead.

Gregorio had worked in the cigar factories, been a sign painter, an ice-cream peddler, and for a short time a photographer, in the effort to support his large family. He made several trips to Cuba and twenty years ago worked for a while in the cigar factories in Tampa, returning to Key West because his wife liked it better. While in Tampa he painted signs as well, and also the sides of delivery wagons. There are some of his signs in Key West—a large one for the

Sociedad de Cuba and one for a grocery store, especially, have certain of the qualities of his pictures. Just down the street from his house, opposite the Sociedad de Cuba, there used to be a little café for the workers in a nearby cigar factory, the Forget-Me-Not Café, *Café no me Olvidades.* Ten years ago or so Gregorio painted a picture of it on the wall of the café itself, with the blue sky, the telephone pole and wires, and the name, all very exact. Mr. Rafael Rodríguez, the former owner, who showed it to us, seemed to feel rather badly because since the cigar factory and the café have both disappeared, the color of the doors and window frames has been changed from blue to orange, making Gregorio's picture no longer as perfect as it was.

This story is told by Mr. Edwin Denby in his article on Valdes for the Artists' Gallery exhibition: "When he was a young man he lived with an uncle. One day when that uncle was at work, Valdes took down the towel rack that hung next to the washbasin and put up instead a painting of the rack with the towel on it. When the uncle came back at five, he went to the basin, bent over and washed his face hard; and still bent over he reached up for the towel. But he couldn't get hold. With the water streaming into his eyes, he squinted up at it, saw it and clawed at it, but the towel wouldn't come off the wall. 'Me laugh plenty, plenty,' Valdes said . . . "

This classical ideal of verisimilitude did not always succeed so well, fortunately. Gregorio was not a great painter at all, and although he certainly belongs to the class of painters we call "primitive," sometimes he was not even a good "primitive." His pictures are of uneven quality. They are almost all copies of photographs or of reproductions of other pictures. Usually when he copied from such reproductions he succeeded in nothing more than the worst sort of "calendar" painting, and again when he copied, particularly from a photograph, and particularly from a photograph of something he knew and liked, such as palm trees, he managed to make just the right changes in perspective and coloring to give it a peculiar and captivating freshness, flatness, and remoteness. But Gregorio himself did not see any difference between what we think of as his good pictures and his poor pictures, and his painting a good one or a bad one seems to have been entirely a matter of luck.

There are some people whom we envy because they are rich or handsome or successful, although they may be any or all of these, but because everything they are and do seems to be all of a piece, so that even if they wanted to they could not be or do otherwise. A particular feature of their characters may stand out as more praiseworthy in itself than others—that is almost beside the point. Ancient heroes often have to do penance for and expiate crimes they have committed all unwittingly, and in the same way it seems that some people receive certain "gifts" merely by remaining unwittingly in an undemocratic state of grace. It is a supposition that leaves painting like Gregorio's a partial mystery. But surely anything that is impossible for others to achieve by effort, that is dangerous to imitate, and yet, like natural virtue, must be both admired and imitated, always remains mysterious.

Anyway, who could fail to enjoy and admire those secretive palm trees in their pink skies, the Traveler's Palm, like "the fan-filamented antenna of a certain gigantic moth . . . " or the picture of the church in Cuba copied from a liquor advertisement and labeled with so literal a translation from the Spanish, "Church of St. Mary Rosario 300 Years Constructed in Cuba."

John Sayles

LOS GUSANOS

THE KILLING OUT front is great for lunch business. Tío Felix has given the girl the day off and so is working the counter himself. Sometimes he still likes to work the counter.

"Chicharrón pollo!" he yells in to Hong. "Carne guisada! Seven-Up!"

They come and stand around the sidewalk looking for stains, arguing about who the boy was and why they had executed him and did he deserve it or not and then they come in to sit at the counter, still arguing, hungry.

"Serrucho frito!" Felix yells in to his old cook. "Yuca y moros. Dos pollo asado!"

John Sayles's innovative, highly acclaimed films include The Return of the Secaucus Seven, Brother from Another Planet, Eight Men Out, *and* City of Hope. *This excerpt is from the filmmaker's first novel,* Los Gusanos, *published in 1991.*

Once he had posted a sign, *Prohibido Discutir de Política en este Restaurante*, but they ignored it. Hong is only a few feet away in the kitchen but Felix has to shout over all the arguing to be heard.

"Bistec salteado!"

"Tío," says Marta, helping him carry plates of fried ham to the end of the counter, "you know somebody. Tell me who."

"Nadie. I know restaurant, I know farmacia, I know newsstand, I know fishing boat. I don know politics."

"What do you talk all day with your friends out at the Big Five?"

"Deportes. Negocios. No política."

"You know someone, Tío. I know you do."

"Felix," calls Salazar, who runs the record store down the street, "sopa mondongo, para llevar. Para mi esposa."

"Sopa mondongo, para llevar!" Tío Felix is sweating already. When Felix works the counter he keeps three extra shirts hanging in the back.

"I don see why they kill him," he says. He nods toward the men arguing over their beans and rice as if they were the ones responsible. "What do they want? Is over. He's sending all the prisoner home."

"Después de quebrantarlos."

Felix points to a small man sitting alone in the corner. "Does he look broken to you?"

Villas sits eating fried fish, gazing out the window. The men who argue lower their voices a little bit when they stand near him.

Marta wonders what he'd say if she came to him with her plan. She looks in his eyes for twenty years in prison.

"You were in the fighting after the Invasion, Tío. They used your boats. You know people."

"No conozco a nadie. The ones who are still in it go under. Nobody knows who they are. The only guy I hear talk that kind of política, I don know him."

When she was younger he could have shut her up with a milkshake. She would come in, head barely over the countertop, laying down whatever little handful of nickels and pennies she had collected. "Batido de mamey, por favor," she would order, and then, politely, "Buenas tardes, Tío." She would be full of questions about why this and why that till the batido was ready. She never got any on her face and when the level in her glass was just right she'd fill it back up from the metal tumbler. She never used a straw, but closed her eyes and drank long and slow like a baby suckling, coming out of it to gasp for air between drinks. Felix would turn to look at her face when she closed her eyes, wondering at how everything was perfect on a small scale, loving how smooth her skin was, wishing for a wife and daughters of his own. He would make a big show of counting her change and ringing it into the register. She never wanted a batido for free, but when he pressed a silver dollar into her hand before she left she didn't complain. "Muchas gracias, Tío," she would say, with the half-curtsy the nuns had taught her.

"Who is he?" asks Marta. "The one who talks politics?"

"Why you want to know?"

"It's my business," says Marta. "Y el de mi padre."

"Felix," calls Padilla, who sells insurance. "Medianoche, chuleta, y dos cervezas. Denos Heineken por favor."

"Espere un momento, compa, espere." Felix has broken the point of his pencil and there are too many orders to keep straight in his head. Men are starting to come in the door, see the crowd, then go back out. He wishes he hadn't given the girl the day off.

"How can it be business for Scipio?" he asks.

"He talks to me. We decide things."

"No habla con nadie. No puede hablar."

"He talks to me." Marta stands blocking his way to the kitchen, tight-mouthed, daring him to challenge her. "We do it without words."

It is expensive for Felix to keep Scipio with the Jews but Marta insists the care is better there. A bed is a bed, thinks Felix, and immediately feels bad.

"Who is the one who talks that kind of politics?"

Marta has him blocked right under the fan. The sweat on his forehead goes cold.

"Nuñez," he says. "Señor Nuñez. He sells magazines. He's not a good man."

"Por qué dices esto?"

Tío Felix blushes. Marta remembers the first time he blushed when she kissed him, when she was just starting eighth grade and came to show him her new uniform. After that she tried to stand farther away.

"Because of the kind of magazine he sells. For the newsstand."

Marta nods. "Sometime," she says, "I may want to borrow one of your boats."

"You don fish."

They are quiet as Villas comes up to pay his bill. Marta tries to look into his eyes but he has put sunglasses on to face the street.

"You don fish," says Felix when the man is gone.

"You let other people use it. They didn't fish."

"That was diff'rent." Felix wishes he had never listened to them. But there was the bank loan and the liquor license and there was Scipio talking in his ear. "That was United States government."

"So? Son más importantes que tu familia?"

"Camarón enchilado," says old Hong, passing a hot plate through his portal. "No hay yuca."

"No. But I don want my family to get in trouble." Felix takes the plate to a man in the front booth, Marta trailing after him.

"You let Blas use it."

Felix looks around nervously. "Who told you that?"

"You did some big deal with him. Lots of money."

"No es verdad. Fué un favor."

"So do me a favor. Let me use a boat."

"For what you want it?"

"I can't tell you."

"I promise to your father—"

"No prometó nada a mi padre!" Marta startles herself with her shout. The men stop to look at her for a second, then go back to eating and arguing.

"When he gave you money to start a business," she says, lowering her voice, "did he ask you how you would use it?"

"Is too dangerous, what you get into, créeme. I been there, sobrina."

"Where? Where have you been? You never fired a shot."

He blushes again, a different kind of blush. "I was ready to," he says.

Hong lays two steaming plates of rice and beans on the portal ledge but Felix can't think of who they are for. The men argue whether there will be more executions. Hong calls out that they are out of Heineken.

"I was ready if I had to," says Tío Felix, touching Marta's arm, looking to her eyes for belief. "I was ready to die."

Stephen Crane

The Open Boat

I

NONE OF THEM knew the color of the sky. Their eyes glanced level, and were fastened upon the waves that swept toward them. These waves were the hue of slate, save for the tops, which were of foaming white, and all of the men knew the colors of the sea. The horizon narrowed and widened and dipped and rose, and at all times its edge was jagged with waves that seemed thrust up in points like rocks.

Many a man ought to have a bath-tub larger than the boat which here rode upon the sea. These waves were most wrongfully

---

Stephen Crane, author of The Red Badge of Courage, *was working as a reporter in 1897 when, en route to Cuba, he was shipwrecked off Daytona Beach. This near-death experience led to his writing of the classic sea-story, "The Open Boat."*

and barbarously abrupt and tall, and each froth-top was a problem in small-boat navigation.

The cook squatted in the bottom, and looked with both eyes at the six inches of gunwale which separated him from the ocean. His sleeves were rolled over his fat forearms, and the two flaps of his unbuttoned vest dangled as he bent to bail out the boat. Often he said. "Gawd! that was a narrow clip." As he remarked it he invariably gazed eastward over the broken sea.

The oiler, steering with one of the two oars in the boat, sometimes raised himself suddenly to keep clear of water that swirled in over the stern. It was a thin little oar, and it seemed often ready to snap.

The correspondent, pulling at the other oar, watched the waves and wondered why he was there.

The injured captain, lying in the bow, was at this time buried in that profound rejection and indifference which comes, temporarily at least, to even the bravest and most enduring when, willy-nilly, the firm fails, the army loses, the ship goes down. The mind of the master of a vessel is rooted deep in the timbers of her, though he command for a day or a decade; and this captain had on him the stern impression of a scene in the grays of dawn of seven turned faces, and later a stump of a topmast with a white ball on it, that slashed to and fro at the waves, went low and lower, and down. Thereafter there was something strange in his voice. Although steady, it was deep with mourning, and of a quality beyond oration or tears.

"Keep'er a little more south, Billie," said he.

"A little more south, sir," said the oiler in the stern.

A seat in this boat was not unlike a seat upon a bucking bronco, and, by the same token, a bronco is not much smaller. The craft pranced and reared and plunged like an animal. As each wave came, and she rose for it, she seemed like a horse making at a fence outrageously high. The manner of her scramble over these walls of water is a mystic thing, and, moreover, at the top of them were ordinarily these problems in white water, the foam racing down from the summit of each wave, requiring a new leap, and a leap from the air. Then, after scornfully bumping a crest, she would slide and race and splash down a long incline, and arrive bobbing and nodding in front of the next menace.

A singular disadvantage of the sea lies in the fact that, after successfully surmounting one wave, you discover that there is another behind it, just as important and just as nervously anxious to do something effective in the way of swamping boats. In a ten-foot dinghy one can get an idea of the resources of the sea in the line of waves that is not probable to the average experience, which is never at sea in a dinghy. As each slaty wall of water approached, it shut all else from the view of the men in the boat, and it was not difficult to imagine that this particular wave was the final outburst of the ocean, the last effort of the grim water. There was a terrible grace in the move of the waves, and they came in silence, save for the snarling of the crests.

In the wan light the faces of the men must have been gray.

Their eyes must have glinted in strange ways as they gazed steadily astern. Viewed from a balcony, the whole thing would, doubtless, have been weirdly picturesque. But the men in the boat had no time to see it, and if they had had leisure, there were other things to occupy their minds. The sun swung steadily up the sky, and they knew it was broad day because the color of the sea changed from slate to emerald-green streaked with amber lights, and the foam was like tumbling snow. The process of the breaking day was unknown to them. They were aware only of this effect upon the color of the waves that rolled toward them.

In disjointed sentences the cook and the correspondent argued as to the difference between a life-saving station and a house of refuge. The cook had said: "There's a house of refuge just north of the Mosquito Inlet Light, and as soon as they see us they'll come off in their boat and pick us up."

"As soon as who see us?" said the correspondent.

"The crew," said the cook.

"Houses of refuge don't have crews," said the correspondent. "As I understand them, they are only places where clothes and grub are stored for the benefit of shipwrecked people. They don't carry crews."

"Oh, yes, they do," said the cook.

"No, they don't," said the correspondent.

"Well, we're not there yet, anyhow," said the oiler in the stern.

"Well," said the cook, "perhaps it's not a house of refuge that

I'm thinking of as being near Mosquito Inlet Light; perhaps it's a life-saving station."

"We're not there yet." said the oiler in the stern.

II

A S T H E B O A T bounced from the top of each wave the wind tore through the hair of the hatless men, and as the craft plopped her stern down again the spray splashed past them. The crest of each of these waves was a hill, from the top of which the men surveyed for a moment a broad, tumultuous expanse, shining and wind-riven. It was probably splendid, it was probably glorious, this play of the free sea, wild with lights of emerald and white and amber.

"Bully good thing it's an on-shore wind," said the cook. "If not, where would we be? Wouldn't have a show."

"That's right," said the correspondent.

The busy oiler nodded his assent.

Then the captain, in the bow, chuckled in a way that expressed humor, contempt, tragedy, all in one. "Do you think we've got much of a show now, boys?" said he.

Whereupon the three were silent, save for a trifle of hemming and hawing. To express any particular optimism at this time they felt to be childish and stupid, but they all doubtless possessed this sense of the situation in their minds. A young man thinks doggedly at such times. On the other hand, the ethics of their condition was decidedly against any open suggestion of hopelessness. So they were silent.

"Oh, well," said the captain, soothing his children, "we'll get ashore all right."

But there was that in his tone which made them think; so the oiler quoth, "Yes! if this wind holds."

The cook was bailing. "Yes! if we don't catch hell in the surf."

Canton-flannel gulls flew near and far. Sometimes they sat down on the sea, near patches of brown seaweed that rolled over the waves with a moment like carpets on a line in a gale. The birds sat comfortably in groups, and they were envied by some in the dinghy, for the wrath of the sea was no more to them than it was to a covey of prairie-chickens a thousand miles inland. Often they came very close and stared at the men with black, bead-like eyes. At these times they were uncanny and sinister in their unblinking scrutiny, and the men hooted angrily at them, telling them to be gone. One came, and evidently decided to alight on the top of the captain's head. The bird flew parallel to the boat, and did not circle, but made short sidelong jumps in the air in chicken fashion. His black eyes were wistfully fixed upon the captain's head. "Ugly brute," said the oiler to the bird. "You look as if you were made with a jack-knife." The cook and the correspondent swore darkly at the creature. The captain naturally wished to knock it away with the end of the heavy painter, but he did not dare do it, because anything resembling an emphatic gesture would have capsized this freighted boat; and so, with his open hand, the captain gently and carefully waved the gull away. After it had been discouraged from the pursuit the captain breathed easier on account of his hair, and others breathed easier because the bird struck their minds at this time as being somehow gruesome and ominous.

In the meantime the oiler and the correspondent rowed; and also they rowed. They sat together in the same seat, and each rowed an oar. Then the oiler took both oars; then the correspondent took both oars; then the oiler; then the correspondent. They rowed and they rowed. The very ticklish part of the business was when the time came for the reclining one in the stern to take his turn at the oars. By the very last star of truth, it is easier to steal eggs from under a hen than it was to change seats in the dinghy. First the man in the stern slid his hand along the thwart and moved with care, as if he were of Sèvres. Then the man in the rowing-seat slid his hand along the other thwart. It was all done with the most extraordinary care. As the two sidled past each other, the whole party kept watchful eyes on the coming wave, and the captain cried: "Look out, now! Steady, there!"

The brown mats of seaweed that appeared from time to time were like islands, bits of earth. They were traveling, apparently, neither one way nor the other. They were, to all intents, stationary. They informed the men in the boat that it was making progress slowly toward the land.

The captain, rearing cautiously in the bow after the dinghy soared on a great swell, said that he had seen the lighthouse at Mosquito Inlet. Presently the cook remarked that he had seen it. The correspondent was at the oars then, and for some reason he too wished to look at the lighthouse; but his back was toward the far shore, and the waves were important, and for some time he could not seize an opportunity to turn his head. But at last there came a wave more gentle than the others, and when at the crest of it he swiftly scoured the western horizon.

"See it?" said the captain.

"No," said the correspondent, slowly; "I didn't see anything."

"Look again," said the captain. He pointed. "It's exactly in that direction."

At the top of another wave the correspondent did as he was bid, and this time his eyes chanced on a small, still thing on the edge of the swaying horizon. It was precisely like the point of a pin. It took an anxious eye to find a lighthouse so tiny.

"Think we'll make it, Captain?"

"If this wind holds and the boat don't swamp, we can't do much else," said the captain.

The little boat, lifted by each towering sea and splashed viciously by the crests, made progress that in the absence of seaweed was not apparent to those in her. She seemed just a wee thing wallow-ing miraculously, top up, at the mercy of five oceans. Occasionally a great spread of water, like white flames, swarmed into her.

"Bail her, cook," said the captain, serenely.

"All right, Captain," said the cheerful cook.

III

IT WOULD BE difficult to describe the subtle brotherhood of men that was here established on the seas. No one said that it was so. No one mentioned it. But it dwelt in the boat, and each man felt it warm

him. They were a captain, an oiler, a cook, and a correspondent, and
they were friends—friends in a more curiously iron-bound degree
than may be common. The hurt captain, lying against the water-jar in
the bow, spoke always in a low voice and calmly; but he could never
command a more ready and swiftly obedient crew than the motley
three of the dinghy. It was more than a mere recognition of what was
best for the common safety. There was surely in it a quality that was
personal and heartfelt. And after this devotion to the commander of
the boat, there was this comradeship, that the correspondent, for
instance, who had been taught to be cynical of men, knew even at the
time was the best experience of his life. But no one said that it was so.
No one mentioned it.

"I wish we had a sail," remarked the captain. "We might try
my overcoat on the end of an oar, and give you two boys a chance to
rest." So the cook and the correspondent held the mast and spread
wide the overcoat; the oiler steered; and the little boat made good way
with her new rig. Sometimes the oiler had to scull sharply to keep a
sea from breaking into the boat, but otherwise sailing was a success.

Meanwhile the lighthouse had been growing slowly larger. It
had now almost assumed color, and appeared like a little gray shadow
on the sky. The man at the oars could not be prevented from turning
his head rather often to try for a glimpse of this little gray shadow.

At last, from the top of each wave, the men in the tossing
boat could see land. Even as the lighthouse was an upright shadow
on the sky, this land seemed but a long black shadow on the sea. It certainly was thinner than paper. "We must be about opposite New

Smyrna," said the cook, who had coasted this shore often in schooners. "Captain, by the way, I believe they abandoned that life-saving station there about a year ago."

"Did they?" said the captain.

The wind slowly died away. The cook and the correspondent were not now obliged to slave in order to hold high the oar; but the waves continued their old impetuous swooping at the dinghy, and the little craft, no longer under way, struggled woundily over them. The oiler or the correspondent took the oars again.

Shipwrecks are *apropos* of nothing. If men could only train for them and have them occur when the men had reached pink condition, there would be less drowning at sea. Of the four in the dinghy none had slept any time worth mentioning for two days and two nights previous to embarking in the dinghy, and in the excitement of clambering about the deck of a foundering ship they had also forgotten to eat heartily.

For these reasons, and for others, neither the oiler nor the correspondent was fond of rowing at this time. The correspondent wondered ingenuously how in the name of all that was sane could there be people who thought it amusing to row a boat. It was not an amusement; it was a diabolical punishment, and even a genius of mental aberrations could never conclude that it was anything but a horror to the muscles and a crime against the back. He mentioned to the boat in general how the amusement of rowing struck him, and the weary-faced oiler smiled in full sympathy. Previously to the foundering, by the way, the oiler had worked double watch in the engine-room of the ship.

"Take her easy now, boys," said the captain. "Don't spend yourselves. If we have to run a surf you'll need all your strength, because we'll sure have to swim for it. Take your time."

Slowly the land arose from the sea. From a black line it became a line of black and a line of white—trees and sand. Finally the captain said that he could make out a house on the shore. "That's the house of refuge, sure," said the cook. "They'll see us before long, and come out after us."

The distant lighthouse reared high. "The keeper ought to be able to make us out now, if he's looking through a glass," said the captain. "He'll notify the life-saving people."

"None of those other boats could have got ashore to give word of the wreck," said the oiler, in a low voice, "else the lifeboat would be out hunting us."

Slowly and beautifully the land loomed out of the sea. The wind came again. It had veered from the northeast to the southeast. Finally a new sound struck the ears of the men in the boat. It was the low thunder of the surf on the shore. "We'll never be able to make the lighthouse now," said the captain. "Swing her head a little more north, Billie."

"A little more north, sir," said the oiler.

Whereupon the little boat turned her nose once more down the wind, and all but the oarsman watched the shore grow. Under the influence of this expansion doubt and direful apprehension were leaving the minds of the men. The management of the boat was still most absorbing, but it could not prevent a quiet cheerfulness. In an hour, perhaps, they would be ashore.

Their backbones had become thoroughly used to balancing in the boat, and they now rode this wild colt of a dinghy like circus men. The correspondent thought that he had been drenched to the skin, but happening to feel in the top pocket of his coat, he found therein eight cigars. Four of them were soaked with sea-water; four were perfectly scatheless. After a search, somebody produced three dry matches; and thereupon the four waifs rode in their little boat and, with an assurance of an impending rescue shining in their eyes, puffed at the big cigars, and judged well and ill of all men. Everybody took a drink of water.

IV

"Cook," remarked the captain, "there don't seem to be any signs of life about your house of refuge."

"No," replied the cook. "Funny they don't see us!"

A broad stretch of lowly coast lay before the eyes of the men. It was of low dunes topped with dark vegetation. The roar of the surf was plain, and sometimes they could see the white lip of a wave as it spun up the beach. A tiny house was blocked out black upon the sky. Southward, the slim lighthouse lifted its little gray length.

Tide, wind, and waves were swinging the dinghy northward. "Funny they don't see us," said the men.

The surf's roar was here dulled, but its tone was nevertheless thunderous and mighty. As the boat swam over the great rollers the men sat listening to this roar. "We'll swamp sure," said everybody.

It is fair to say here that there was not a life-saving station within twenty miles in either direction; but the men did not know this fact, and in consequence they made dark and approbrious remarks concerning the eyesight of the nation's life-savers. Four scowling men sat in the dinghy, and surpassed records in the invention of epithets.

"Funny they don't see us."

The light-heartedness of a former time had completely faded. To their sharpened minds it was easy to conjure pictures of all kinds of incompetency and blindness and, indeed, cowardice. There was the shore of the populous land, and it was bitter and bitter to them that from it came no sign.

"Well," said the captain, ultimately, "I suppose we'll have to make a try for ourselves. If we stay out here too long, we'll none of us have strength left to swim after the boat swamps."

And so the oiler, who was at the oars, turned the boat straight for the shore. There was a sudden tightening of muscles. There was some thinking.

"If we don't all get ashore," said the captain—"if we don't all get ashore, I suppose you fellows know where to send news of my finish?"

They then briefly exchanged some addresses and admonitions. As for the reflections of the men, there was a great deal of rage in them. Perchance they might be formulated thus: "If I am going to be drowned—if I am going to be drowned—if I am going to be drowned, why, in the name of the seven mad gods who rule the sea, was I allowed to come thus far and contemplate sand and trees? Was I brought here merely to have my nose dragged away as I was about to nibble the sacred cheese of life? It is preposterous! If this old ninny-woman, Fate, cannot do better than this, she could be deprived of the management of men's fortunes. She is an old hen who knows not her intention. If she has decided to drown men, why did she not do it in the beginning, and save me all this trouble? The whole affair is absurd. . . . But no; she cannot mean to drown me. She dare not drown men. She cannot drown me. Not after all this work!" Afterward the man might have had an impulse to shake his fist at the clouds. "Just you drown me, now, and then hear what I call you!"

The billows that came at this time were more formidable. They seemed always just about to break and roll over the little boat in turmoil of foam. There was a preparatory and long growl in the speech of them. No mind unused to the sea would have concluded that the dinghy could ascend these sheer heights in time. The shore was still afar. The oiler was a wily surfman. "Boys," he said swiftly, "she won't live three minutes more, and we're too far out to swim. Shall I take her to sea again, Captain?"

"Yes; go ahead!" said the captain.

This oiler, by a series of quick miracles and fast and steady oarsmanship, turned the boat in the middle of the surf and took her safely to sea again.

There was a considerable silence as the boat bumped over the furrowed sea to deeper water. Then somebody in gloom spoke: "Well, anyhow, they must have seen us from shore by now."

The gulls went in slanting flight up the wind toward the gray, desolate east. A squall, marked by dingy clouds, and clouds brick-red, like smoke from a burning building, appeared from the southeast.

"What do you think of those life-saving people? Ain't they peaches?"

"Funny they haven't seen us."

"Maybe they think we're out here for sport! Maybe they think we're fishin'. Maybe they think we're damned fools."

It was a long afternoon. A changed tide tried to force them southward, but wind and wave said northward. Far ahead, where coast-line, sea, and sky formed their mighty angle, there were little dots which seemed to indicate a city on the shore.

"St. Augustine?"

The captain shook his head. "Too near Mosquito Inlet."

And the oiler rowed, and then the correspondent rowed; then the oiler rowed. It was a weary business. The human back can become the seat of more aches and pains than are registered in books for the composite anatomy of a regiment. It is a limited area, but it can become the theater of innumerable muscular conflicts, tangles, wrenches, knots, and other comforts.

"Did you ever like to row, Billie?" asked the correspondent.

"No," said the oiler; "hang it!"

When one exchanged the rowing-seat for a place in the bottom of the boat, he suffered a bodily depression that caused him to be careless of everything save an obligation to wiggle one finger. There was cold sea-water swashing to and fro in the boat, and he lay in it. His head, pillowed on a thwart, was within an inch of the swirl of a wave-crest, and sometimes a particularly obstreperous sea came inboard and drenched him once more. But these matters did not annoy him. It is almost certain that if the boat had capsized he would have tumbled comfortably out upon the ocean as if he felt sure that it was a great, soft mattress.

"Look! There's a man on the shore!"

"Where?"

"There! See 'im? See 'im?"

"Yes, sure! He's walking along."

"Now he's stopped. Look! He's facing us!"

"He's waving at us!"

"So he is! By thunder!"

"Ah, now we're all right! Now we're all right! There'll be a boat out here for us in half an hour."

"He's going on. He's running. He's going up to that house there."

The remote beach seemed lower than the sea, and it required a searching glance to discern the little black figure. The captain saw a floating stick, and they rowed to it. A bath towel was by some weird chance in the boat, and tying this on the stick, the captain waved it. The oarsman did not dare turn his head, so he was obliged to ask questions.

"What's he doing now?"

"He's standing still again. He's looking, I think. . . . There he goes again—toward the house. . . . Now he's stopped again."

"Is he waving at us?"

"No, not now; he was though."

"Look! There comes another man!"

"He's running."

"Look at him go, would you!"

"Why, he's on a bicycle. Now he's met the other man. They're both waving at us. Look!"

"There comes something up the beach."

"What the devil is that thing?"

"Why, it looks like a boat."

"Why, certainly, it's a boat."

"No; it's on wheels."

"Yes, so it is. Well, that must be the life-boat. They drag them along shore on a wagon."

"That's the life-boat, sure."

"No, by—, it's—it's an omnibus."

"I tell you it's a life-boat."

"It is not! It's an omnibus. I can see it plain. See? One of these big hotel omnibuses."

"By thunder, you're right. It's an omnibus, sure as fate. What do you suppose they are doing with an omnibus? Maybe they are going around collecting the life-crew, hey?"

"That's it, likely. Look! There's a fellow waving a little black flag. He's standing on the steps of the omnibus. There come those other two fellows. Now they're all talking together. Look at the fellow with the flag. Maybe he ain't waving it!"

"That ain't a flag, is it? That's his coat. Why, certainly, that's his coat."

"So it is; it's his coat. He's taken it off and is waving it around his head. But would you look at him swing it!"

"Oh, say, there isn't any life-saving station there. That's just a winter-resort hotel omnibus that has brought over some of the boarders to see us drown."

"What's that idiot with the coat mean? What's he signaling, anyhow?"

"It looks as if he were trying to tell us to go north. There must be a life-saving station up there."

"No; he thinks we're fishing. Just giving us a merry hand. See? Ah, there, Willie!"

"Well, I wish I could make something out of those signals. What do you suppose he means?"

"He don't mean anything; he's just playing."

"Well, if he'd just signal us to try the surf again, or to go to sea and wait, or go north, or go south, or go to hell, there would be some reason in it. But look at him! He just stands there and keeps his coat revolving like a wheel. The ass!"

"There comes more people."

"Now there's quite a mob. Look! Isn't that a boat?"

"Where? Oh, I see where you mean. No, that's no boat."

"That fellow is still waving his coat."

"He must think we like to see him do that. Why don't he quit it? It don't mean anything."

"I don't know. I think he is trying to make us go north. It must be that there's a life-saving station there somewhere."

"Say, he ain't tired yet. Look at 'im wave!"

"Wonder how long he can keep that up. He's been revolving his coat ever since he caught sight of us. He's an idiot. Why aren't they getting men to bring a boat out? A fishing-boat—one of those big yawls—could come out here all right. Why don't he do something?"

"Oh, it's all right now."

"They'll have a boat out here for us in less than no time, now that they've seen us."

A faint yellow tone came into the sky over the low land. The shadows on the sea slowly deepened. The wind bore coldness with it, and the men began to shiver.

"Holy smoke!" said one, allowing his voice to express his impious mood, "if we keep on monkeying out here! If we've got to flounder out here all night!"

"Oh, we'll never have to stay here all night! Don't you worry. They've seen us now, and it won't be long before they'll come chasing out after us."

The shore grew dusky. The man waving a coat blended gradually into this gloom, and it swallowed in the same manner the omnibus and the group of people. The spray, when it dashed uproariously over the side, made the voyagers shrink and swear like men who were being branded.

"I'd like to catch the chump who waved the coat. I feel like soaking him one, just for luck."

"Why? What did he do?"

"Oh, nothing, but then he seemed so damned cheerful."

In the meantime the oiler rowed, and then the correspondent rowed, and then the oiler rowed. Gray-faced and bowed forward, they mechanically, turn by turn, plied the leaden oars. The form of the lighthouse had vanished from the southern horizon, but finally a pale star appeared, just lifting from the sea. The streaked saffron in the west passed before the all-merging darkness, and the sea to the east was black. The land had vanished, and was expressed only by the low and drear thunder of the surf.

"If I am going to be drowned—if I am going to be drowned—if I am going to be drowned, why, in the name of the seven mad gods who rule the sea, was I allowed to come thus far and contemplate sand and trees? Was I brought here merely to have my nose dragged away as I was about to nibble the sacred cheese of life?"

The patient captain, drooped over the water-jar, was sometimes obliged to speak to the oarsman.

"Keep her head up! Keep her head up!"

"Keep her head up, sir." The voices were weary and low.

This was surely a quiet evening. All save the oarsman lay heavily and listlessly in the boat's bottom. As for him, his eyes were just capable of noting the tall black waves that swept forward in a most sinister silence, save for an occasional subdued growl of a crest.

The cook's head was on a thwart, and he looked without interest at the water under his nose. He was deep in other scenes. Finally he spoke. "Billie," he murmured dreamfully, "what kind of pie do you like best?"

V

"PIE!" SAID THE oiler and the correspondent, agitatedly. "Don't talk about those things, blast you!"

"Well," said the cook, "I was just thinking about ham sand-wiches, and—"

A night on the sea in an open boat is a long night. As dark-ness settled finally, the shine of the light, lifting from the sea in the south, changed to full gold. On the northern horizon a new light appeared, a small bluish gleam on the edge of the waters. These two lights were the furniture of the world. Otherwise there was nothing but waves.

Two men huddled in the stern, and distances were so magnif-icent in the dinghy that the rower was enabled to keep his feet partly warm by thrusting them under his companions. Their legs indeed extended far under the rowing-seat until they touched the feet of the captain forward. Sometimes, despite the efforts of the tired oarsman, a wave came piling into the boat, an icy wave of the night, and the chilling water soaked them anew. They would twist their bodies for a moment and groan, and sleep the dead sleep once more, while the water in the boat gurgled about them as the craft rocked.

The plan of the oiler and the correspondent was for one to

row until he lost the ability, and then arouse the other from his sea-water couch in the bottom of the boat.

The oiler plied his oars until his head drooped forward and the overpowering sleep blinded him; and he rowed yet afterward. Then he touched a man in the bottom of the boat, and called his name. "Will you spell me for a little while?" he said meekly.

"Sure, Billie," said the correspondent, awaking and dragging himself to a sitting position. They exchanged places carefully, and the oiler, cuddling down in the sea-water at the cook's side, seemed to go to sleep instantly.

The particular violence of the sea had ceased. The waves came without snarling. The obligation of the man at the oars was to keep the boat headed so that the tilt of the rollers would not capsize her, and to preserve her from filling when the crests rushed past. The black waves were silent and hard to be seen in the darkness. Often one was almost upon the boat before the oarsman was aware.

In a low voice the correspondent addressed the captain. He was not sure that the captain was awake, although this iron man seemed to be always awake. "Captain, shall I keep her making for that light north, sir?"

The same steady voice answered him. "Yes. Keep it about two points off the port bow."

The cook had tied a life-belt around himself in order to get even the warmth which this clumsy cork contrivance could donate, and he seemed almost stove-like when a rower, whose teeth invariably chattered wildly as soon as he ceased to labor, dropped down to sleep.

The correspondent, as he rowed, looked down at the two men sleeping under foot. The cook's arm was around the oiler's shoulders, and, with their fragmentary clothing and haggard faces, they were the babes of the sea—a grotesque rendering of the old babes in the wood.

Later he must have grown stupid at his work, for suddenly there was a growling of water, and a crest came with a roar and a swash into the boat, and it was a wonder that it did not set the cook afloat in his life-belt. The cook continued to sleep, but the oiler sat up, blinking his eyes and shaking with the new cold.

"Oh, I'm awful sorry, Billie" said the correspondent, contritely.

"That's all right, old boy," said the oiler, and lay down again and was asleep.

Presently it seemed that even the captain dozed, and the correspondent thought that he was the one man afloat on all the oceans. The wind had a voice as it came over the waves, and it was sadder than the end.

There was a long, loud swishing astern of the boat, and a gleaming trail of phosphorescence, like blue flame, was furrowed on the black waters. It might have been made by a monstrous knife.

Then there came a stillness, while the correspondent breathed with the open mouth and looked at the sea.

Suddenly there was another swish and another long flash of bluish light, and this time it was alongside the boat, and might almost have been reached with an oar. The correspondent saw an enormous fin speed like a shadow through the water, hurling the crystalline spray and leaving the long glowing trail.

The correspondent looked over his shoulder at the captain. His face was hidden, and he seemed to be asleep. He looked at the babes of the sea. They certainly were asleep. So, being bereft of sympathy, he leaned a little way to one side and swore softly into the sea.

But the thing did not then leave the vicinity of the boat. Ahead or astern, on one side or the other, at intervals long or short, fled the long sparkling streak, and there was to be heard the whiroo of the dark fin. The speed and power of the thing was greatly to be admired. It cut the water like a gigantic and keen projectile.

The presence of this biding thing did not affect the man with the same horror that it would if he had been a picnicker. He simply looked at the sea dully and swore in an undertone.

Nevertheless, it is true that he did not wish to be alone with the thing. He wished one of his companions to awake by chance and keep him company with it. But the captain hung motionless over the water-jar, and the oiler and the cook in the bottom of the boat were plunged in slumber.

VI

"IF I AM going to be drowned—if I am going to be drowned—if I am going to be drowned, why, in the name of the seven mad gods who rule the sea, was I allowed to come thus far and contemplate sand and trees?"

During this dismal night, it may be remarked that a man would conclude that it was really the intention of the seven mad gods to drown him, despite the abominable injustice of it. For it was certainly an abominable injustice to drown a man who had worked so hard, so hard. The man felt it would be a crime most unnatural. Other people had drowned at sea since galleys swarmed with painted sails, but still—

When it occurs to a man that nature does not regard him as important, and that she feels she would not maim the universe by ͺ posing of him, he at first wishes to throw bricks at the temple, and he hates deeply the fact that there are no bricks and no temples. Any visible expression of nature would surely be pelleted with his jeers.

Then, if there be no tangible thing to hoot, he feels, perhaps, the desire to confront a personification and indulge in pleas, bowed to one knee, and with hands supplicant, saying, "Yes, but I love myself."

A high cold star on a winter's night is the word he feels that she says to him. Thereafter he knows the pathos of his situation.

The men in the dinghy had not discussed these matters, but each had, no doubt, reflected upon them in silence and according to his mind. There was seldom any expression upon their faces save the general one of complete weariness. Speech was devoted to the business of the boat.

To chime the notes of his emotion, a verse mysteriously entered the correspondent's head. He had even forgotten that he had forgotten this verse, but it suddenly was in his mind:

A soldier of the Legion lay dying in Algiers;
There was lack of woman's nursing, there was dearth of
  woman's tears;
But a comrade stood beside him, and he took that comrade's
  hand,
And he said, "I never more shall see my own, my native land."

In his childhood the correspondent had been made acquainted with the fact that a soldier of the Legion lay dying in Algiers, but he had never regarded it as important. Myriads of his school-fellows had informed him of the soldier's plight, but the dinning had naturally ended by making him perfectly indifferent. He had never considered it his affair that a soldier of the Legion lay dying in Algiers, nor had it appeared to him as a matter for sorrow. It was less to him than breaking of a pencil's point.

Now, however, it quaintly came to him as a human, living thing. It was no longer merely a picture of a few throes in the breast of a poet, meanwhile drinking tea and warming his feet at the grate; it was an actuality—stern, mournful, and fine.

The correspondent plainly saw the soldier. He lay on the sand with his feet out straight and still. While his pale left hand was upon his chest in an attempt to thwart the going of his life, the blood came between his fingers. In the far Algerian distance, a city of low square forms was set against a sky that was faint with the last sunset hues. The correspondent, plying the oars and dreaming of the slow and slower movements of the lips of the soldier, was moved by a profound and perfectly impersonal comprehension. He was sorry for the soldier of the Legion who lay dying in Algiers.

The thing which had followed the boat and waited had evidently grown bored at the delay. There was no longer to be heard the slash of the cutwater, and there was no longer the flame of the long trail. The light in the north still glimmered, but it was apparently no nearer to the boat. Sometimes the boom of the surf rang in the correspondent's ears, and he turned the craft seaward then and rowed harder. Southward, some one had evidently built a watch-fire on the beach. It was too low and too far to be seen, but it made a shimmering, roseate reflection upon the bluff back of it, and this could be discerned from the boat. The wind came stronger, and sometimes a wave suddenly raged out like a mountain-cat, and there was to be seen the sheen and sparkle of a broken crest.

The captain, in the bow, moved on his water-jar and sat erect. "Pretty long night," he observed to the correspondent. He looked at the shore. "Those life-saving people take their time."

"Did you see that shark playing around?"

"Yes, I saw him. He was a big fellow, all right."

"Wish I had known you were awake."

Later the correspondent spoke into the bottom of the boat.

"Billie!" There was a slow and gradual disentanglement. "Billie, will you spell me?"

"Sure," said the oiler.

As soon as the correspondent touched the cold, comfortable sea-water in the bottom of the boat and had huddled close to the cook's life-belt he was deep in sleep, despite the fact that his teeth played all the popular airs. This sleep was so good to him that it was but a moment before he heard a voice call his name in a tone that demonstrated the last stages of exhaustion. "Will you spell me?"

"Sure, Billie."

The light in the north had mysteriously vanished, but the correspondent took his course from the wide-awake captain.

Later in the night they took the boat farther to sea, and the captain directed the cook to take one oar at the stern and keep the boat facing the seas. He was to call out if he should hear the thunder of the surf. This plan enabled the oiler and the correspondent to get respite together. "We'll give those boys a chance to get into shape again," said the captain. They curled down and, after a few preliminary chatterings and trembles, slept once more the dead sleep. Neither knew they had bequeathed to the cook the company of another shark, or perhaps the same shark.

As the boat caroused on the waves, spray occasionally bumped over the side and gave them a fresh soaking, but this had no power to break their repose. The ominous slash of the wind and the water affected them as it would have affected mummies.

"Boys," said the cook, with the notes of every reluctance in his voice, "she's drifted in pretty close. I guess one of you had better take her to sea again." The correspondent, aroused, heard the crash of the toppled crests.

As he was rowing, the captain gave him some whisky and water, and this steadied the chills out of him. "If I ever get ashore and anybody shows me even a photograph of an oar—"

At last there was a short conversation.

"Billie!... Billie, will you spell me?"

"Sure," said the other.

VII

WHEN THE CORRESPONDENT again opened his eyes, the sea and the sky were each of the gray hue of the dawning. Later, carmine and gold was painted upon the waters. The morning appeared finally, in its splendor, with a sky of pure blue, and the sunlight flamed on the tips of the waves.

On the distant dunes were set many little black cottages, and a tall white windmill reared above them. No man, nor dog, nor bicycle appeared on the beach. The cottages might have formed a deserted village.

The voyagers scanned the shore. A conference was held in the boat. "Well," said the captain, "if no help is coming, we might better try a run through the surf right away. If we stay out here much longer we will be too weak to do anything for ourselves at all." The others silently acquiesced in this reasoning. The boat was headed for the beach. The correspondent wondered if none ever ascended the tall wind-tower, and if then they never looked seaward. This tower was a giant, standing with its back to the plight of the ants. It represented in a degree, to the correspondent, the serenity of nature amid the struggles of the individual—nature in the wind, and nature in the vision of men. She did not seem cruel to him then, nor beneficent, nor treacherous, nor wise. But she was indifferent, flatly indifferent. It is, perhaps, plausible that a man in this situation, impressed with the unconcern of the universe, should see the innumerable flaws of his life and have them taste wickedly in his mind and wish for another chance. A distinction between right and wrong seems absurdly clear to him, then, in this new ignorance of the grave-edge, and he understands that if he were given another opportunity he would mend his conduct and his words, and be better and brighter during an introduction or at a tea.

"Now, boys," said the captain, "she is going to swamp sure. All we can do is to work her in as far as possible, and then when she swamps, pile out and scramble for the beach. Keep cool now, and don't jump until she swamps sure."

The oiler took the oars. Over his shoulders he scanned the surf. "Captain," he said, "I think I'd better bring her about, and keep her head-on to the seas, and back her in."

"All right, Billie," said the captain. "Back her in." The oiler swung the boat then, and, seated in the stern, the cook and the correspondent were obliged to look over their shoulders to contemplate the lonely and indifferent shore.

The monstrous inshore rollers heaved the boat high until the men were again enabled to see the white sheets of water scudding up the slanted beach. "We won't get in very close," said the captain. Each time a man could wrest his attention from the rollers, he turned his glance toward the shore, and in the expression of the eyes during this contemplation there was a singular quality. The correspondent, observing the others, knew that they were not afraid, but the full meaning of their glances was shrouded.

As for himself, he was too tired to grapple fundamentally with the fact. He tried to coerce his mind into thinking of it, but the mind was dominated at this time by the muscles, and the muscles said they did not care. It merely occurred to him that if he should drown it would be a shame.

There were no hurried words, no pallor, no plain agitation. The men simply looked at the shore. "Now, remember to get well clear of the boat when you jump," said the captain.

Seaward the crest of a roller suddenly fell with a thunderous crash, and the long white comber came roaring down upon the boat.

"Steady now," said the captain. The men were silent. They turned their eyes from the shore to the comber and waited. The boat slid up the incline, leaped at the furious top, bounced over it, and swung down the long back of the wave. Some water had been shipped, and the cook bailed it out.

But the next crest crashed also. The tumbling, boiling flood of white water caught the boat and whirled it almost perpendicular. Water swarmed in from all sides. The correspondent had his hands on the gunwale at this time, and when the water entered at that place he swiftly withdrew his fingers, as if he objected to wetting them.

The little boat, drunken with this weight of water, reeled and snuggled deeper into the sea.

"Bail her out, cook! Bail her out!" said the captain.

"All right, Captain," said the cook.

"Now, boys, the next one will do for us sure," said the oiler. "Mind to jump clear of the boat."

The third wave moved forward, huge, furious, implacable. It fairly swallowed the dinghy, and almost simultaneously the men tumbled into the sea. A piece of life-belt had lain in the bottom of the boat, and as the correspondent went overboard he held this to his chest with his left hand.

The January water was icy, and he reflected immediately, that it was colder than he had expected to find it off the coast of Florida. This appeared to his dazed mind as a fact important enough to be noted at the time. The coldness of the water was sad; it was tragic. This fact was somehow mixed and confused with his opinion of his own situation so that it seemed almost a proper reason for tears. The water was cold.

When he came to the surface he was conscious of little but the noisy water. Afterward he saw his companions in the sea. The oiler was ahead in the race. He was swimming strongly and rapidly. Off to the correspondent's left, the cook's great white and corked back bulged out of the water; and in the rear the captain was hanging with his one good hand to the keel of the overturned dinghy.

There is a certain immovable quality to a shore, and the correspondent wondered at it amid the confusion of the sea.

It seemed also very attractive; but the correspondent knew that it was a long journey, and he paddled leisurely. The piece of life-preserver lay under him, and sometimes he whirled down the incline of a wave as if he were on a hand-sled.

But finally he arrived at a place in the sea where travel was beset with difficulty. He did not pause swimming to inquire what manner of current had caught him, but there his progress ceased. The shore was set before him like a bit of scenery on a stage, and he looked at it, and understood with his eyes each detail of it.

As the cook passed, much farther to the left, the captain was calling to him. "Turn over on your back, cook! Turn over on your back and use the oar."

"All right, sir." The cook turned on his back, and paddling with an oar, went ahead as if he were a canoe.

Presently the boat also passed to the left of the correspondent, with the captain clinging with one hand to the keel. He would have appeared like a man raising himself to look over a board fence if it were not for the extraordinary gymnastics of the boat. The correspondent marveled that the captain could still hold to it.

They passed on nearer to shore,—the oiler, the cook, the captain,—and following them went the water-jar, bouncing gaily over the seas.

The correspondent remained in the grip of this strange new enemy, a current. The shore, with its white slope of sand and its green bluff, topped with little silent cottages, was spread like a picture before him. It was very near to him then, but he was impressed as one who, in a gallery, looks at a scene from Brittany or Algiers.

He thought: "I am going to drown? Can it be possible? Can it be possible? Can it be possible?" Perhaps an individual must consider his own death to be the final phenomenon of nature.

But later a wave perhaps whirled him out of this small deadly current, for he found suddenly that he could again make progress toward the shore. Later still he was aware that the captain, clinging with one hand to the keel of the dinghy, had his face turned away from the shore and toward him, and was calling his name. "Come to the boat! Come to the boat!"

In his struggle to reach the captain and the boat, he reflected that when one gets properly wearied drowning must really be a comfortable arrangement—a cessation of hostilities accompanied by a large degree of relief; and he was glad of it, for the main thing in his mind for some moments had been horror of the temporary agony; he did not wish to be hurt.

Presently he saw a man running along the shore. He was undressing with most remarkable speed. Coat, trousers, shirt, everything flew magically off him.

"Come to the boat!" called the captain.

"All right, Captain." As the correspondent paddled, he saw the captain let himself down to bottom and leave the boat. Then the correspondent performed his one little marvel of the voyage. A large wave caught him and flung him with ease and supreme speed completely over the boat and far beyond it. It struck him even then as an event in gymnastics and a true miracle of the sea. An overturned boat in the surf is not a plaything to a swimming man.

The correspondent arrived in water that reached only to his waist, but his condition did not enable him to stand for more than a moment. Each wave knocked him into a heap, and the undertow pulled at him.

Then he saw the man who had been running and undressing, and undressing and running, come bounding into the water. He dragged ashore the cook, and then waded toward the captain; but the captain waved him away and sent him to the correspondent. He was naked—naked as a tree in winter; but a halo was about his head, and he shone like a saint. He gave a strong pull, and a long drag, and a bully heave at the correspondent's hand. The correspondent, schooled in the minor formulæ, said, "Thanks, old man." But suddenly the man cried, "What's that?" He pointed a swift finger. The correspondent said, "Go."

In the shallows, face downward, lay the oiler. His forehead touched sand that was periodically, between each wave, clear of the sea.

The correspondent did not know all that transpired afterward. When he achieved safe ground he fell, striking the sand with each particular part of his body. It was as if he had dropped from a roof, but the thud was grateful to him.

It seems that instantly the beach was populated with men with blankets, clothes, and flasks, and women with coffee-pots and all the remedies sacred to their minds. The welcome of the land to the men from the sea was warm and generous; but a still and dripping shape was carried slowly up the beach, and the land's welcome for it could only be the different and sinister hospitality of the grave.

When it came night, the white waves paced to and fro in the moonlight, and the wind brought the sound of the great sea's voice to the men on shore, and they felt that they could then be interpreters.

Isaac Bashevis Singer

ALONE

WHEN YOU ARE alone, how long the day can be! I read a book and two newspapers, drank a cup of coffee in a cafeteria, worked a cross-word puzzle. I stopped at a store that auctioned Oriental rugs, went into another where Wall Street stocks were sold. True, I was on Collins Avenue in Miami Beach, but I felt like a ghost, cut off from everything. I went into the library and asked a question—the librarian grew frightened. I was like a man who had died, whose space had already been filled. I passed many hotels, each with its special decorations and attractions. The palm trees were topped by half-wilted fans of leaves, and their coconuts hung like heavy testicles. Everything seemed motionless, even the shiny new automobiles gliding over the

---

Yiddish novelist Isaac Bashevis Singer was the author of The Magic of Lublim, Spinoza of Market Street, *and* The Family Mokat. *He was the recipient of a Nobel Prize and two National Book Awards. This 1962 short story takes place in Miami Beach, where Singer moved in 1973.*

asphalt. Every object continued its existence with that effortless force which is, perhaps, the essence of all being.

I bought a magazine, but was unable to read past the first few lines. Getting on a bus, I let myself be taken aimlessly over causeways, islands with ponds, streets lined with villas. The inhabitants, building on a wasteland, had planted trees and flowering plants from all parts of the world; they had filled up shallow inlets along the shore; they had created architectural wonders and had worked out elaborate schemes for pleasure. A planned hedonism. But the boredom of the desert remained. No loud music could dispel it, no garishness wipe it out. We passed a cactus plant whose blades and dusty needles had brought forth a red flower. We rode near a lake surrounded by groups of flamingos airing their wings, and the water mirrored their long beaks and pink feathers. An assembly of birds. Wild ducks flew about, quacking—the swampland refused to give way.

I looked out the open window of the bus. All that I saw was new, yet it appeared old and weary: grandmothers with dyed hair and rouged cheeks, girls in bikinis barely covering their shame, tanned young men guzzling Coca-Cola on water skis.

An old man lay sprawled on the deck of a yacht, warming his rheumatic legs, his white-haired chest open to the sun. He smiled wanly. Nearby, the mistress to whom he had willed his fortune picked at her toes with red fingernails, as certain of her charms as that the sun would rise tomorrow. A dog stood at the stern, gazing haughtily at the yacht's wake, yawning.

It took a long time to reach the end of the line. Once there, I got on another bus. We rode past a pier where freshly caught fish were being weighed. Their bizarre colors, gory skin wounds, glassy eyes, mouths full of congealed blood, sharp-pointed teeth—all were evidence of a wickedness as deep as the abyss. Men gutted fishes with an unholy joy. The bus passed a snake farm, a monkey colony. I saw houses eaten up by termites and a pond of brackish water in which the descendants of the primeval snake crawled and slithered. Parrots screeched with strident voices. At times, strange smells blew in through the bus window, stenches so dense they made my head throb.

Thank God the summer day is shorter in the South than in the North. Evening fell suddenly, without any dusk. Over the lagoons and highways, so thick no light could penetrate, hovered a jungle darkness. Automobiles, headlamps on, slid forward. The moon emerged extraordinarily large and red; it hung in the sky like a geographer's globe bearing a map not of this world. The night had an aura of miracle and cosmic change. A hope I had never forsaken awoke in me: Was I destined to witness an upheaval in the solar system? Perhaps the moon was about to fall down. Perhaps the earth, tearing itself out of its orbit around the sun, would wander into new constellations.

The bus meandered through unknown regions until it returned to Lincoln Road and the fancy stores, half-empty in summer but still stocked with whatever a rich tourist might desire—an ermine wrap, a chinchilla collar, a twelve-carat diamond, an original Picasso drawing. The dandified salesmen, sure in their knowledge that beyond nirvana pulses karma, conversed among themselves in their air-conditioned interiors. I wasn't hungry; nevertheless, I went into a restaurant where a waitress with a newly bleached permanent served me a full meal, quietly and without fuss. I gave her a half-dollar. When I left, my stomach ached and my head was heavy. The late-evening air, baked by the sun, choked me as I came out. On a nearby building a neon sign flashed the temperature—it was ninety-six, and the humidity almost as much! I didn't need a weatherman. Already, lightning flared in the glowing sky, although I didn't hear thunder. A huge cloud was descending from above, thick as a mountain, full of fire and of water. Single drops of rain hit my bald head. The palm trees looked petrified, expecting the onslaught. I hurried back toward my empty hotel, wanting to get there before the rain; besides, I hoped some mail had come for me. But I had covered barely half the distance when the storm broke. One gush and I was drenched as if by a huge wave. A fiery rod lit up the sky and, the same moment, I heard the thunder crack—a sign the lightning was near me. I wanted to run inside somewhere, but chairs blown from nearby porches somersaulted in front of me, blocking my way. Signs were falling down. The top of a palm tree, torn off by the wind, careened past my feet. I saw a second palm tree sheathed in sackcloth, bent to the wind, ready to kneel. In my confusion I kept on running. Sinking into puddles so deep I almost drowned, I rushed forward with the lightness of boyhood. The danger had made me daring, and I screamed and sang, shouting to the storm in its own key. By this time all traffic had stopped, even the automobiles had been abandoned. But I ran on, determined to escape such madness or else go under. I had to get that special-delivery letter, which no one had written and I never received.

I still don't know how I recognized my hotel. I entered the lobby and stood motionless for a few moments, dripping water on the rug. In the mirror across the room, my half-dissolved image reflected itself like a figure in a cubist painting. I managed to get to the elevator and ride up to the third floor. The door of my room stood ajar: inside, mosquitoes, moths, fireflies, and gnats fluttered and buzzed about, sheltering from the storm. The wind had torn down the mosquito net and scattered the papers I had left on the table. The rugs were soaked. I walked over to the window and looked at the ocean. The waves rose like mountains in the middle of seas—monstrous billows ready once and for all to overflow the shores and float the land away. The waters roared with spite and sprayed white foam into the darkness of the night. The waves were barking at the Creator like packs of hounds. With all the strength I had left, I pulled the window down and lowered the blind. I squatted to put my wet books and manuscripts in order. I was hot. Sweat poured from my body, mingling with rivulets of rain water. I peeled off my clothes and they lay near my feet like shells. I felt like a creature who has just emerged from a cocoon.

William Bartram

". . . BEHOLD HIM," HE writes, "rushing forth from the flags and reeds. His enormous body swells. His plaited tail brandished high, floats upon the lake. The waters like a cataract descend from his opening jaws. Clouds of smoke issue from his dilated nostrils. The earth trembles with his thunder. When immediately from the oppo-site coast of the lagoon, emerges from the deep his rival champion. They suddenly dart upon each other. The boiling surface of the lake marks their rapid course, and a terrific conflict commences. They now sink to the bottom folded together in horrid wreaths. The water becomes thick and discoloured. Again they rise, their jaws clap together, re-echoing through the deep surrounding forests. Again they sink, when the contest ends at the muddy bottom of the lake,

---

William Bartram accompanied his botanist dad on a 1765 canoe exploration of the St. Johns River. He seemed obsessed by one of the river's inhabitants: this description of the "greedy, subtle alligator" is from his 1790 notebooks.

and the vanquished makes a hazardous escape, hiding himself in the muddy turbulent waters and sedge on a distant shore. The proud victor exulting returns to the place of action. The shores and forests resound his dreadful roar, together with the triumphing shouts of the plaited tribes around, witnesses of the horrid combat. . . . " And again, "I . . . furnished myself with a club for my defence and went on board . . . but ere I had half-way reached the place, I was attacked on all sides, several endeavouring to overset the canoe. My situation now became precarious to the last degree: two very large ones attacked me closely, at the same instant, rushing up with their heads and part of their bodies above the water, roaring terribly and belching floods of water over me. They struck their jaws together so close to my ears, as almost to stun me, and I expected every moment to be dragged out of the boat and instantly devoured. But I applied my weapon so effectually about me, though at random, that I was so successful as to beat them off a little. . . . I . . . made good my entrance into the lagoon, though not without opposition from the alligators, who formed a line across the entrance, but did not pursue me into it, nor was I molested by any there, though there were some very large ones in a cove at the upper end. I soon caught more trout than I had present occasion for . . . " Bartram then goes on to relate how he was pursued by a daring old alligator about twelve foot in length, and he proceeds, ". . . and when I stepped on shore and turned about, in order to draw up my canoe, he rushed up near my feet, and lay there for some time, looking me in the face, his head and shoulders out of water. I resolved he should pay for his temerity, and having a heavy load in my fuse, I ran to my camp, and returning with my piece, found him with his foot on the gunwale of the boat, in search of fish. On my coming up he withdrew sullenly and slowly into the water, but soon returned and placed himself in his former position, looking at me, and seeming neither fearful nor any way disturbed. I soon despatched him by lodging the contents of my gun in his head, and then proceeded to cleanse and prepare my fish for supper . . . when, raising my head, I saw before me, through the clear water, the head and shoulders of a very large alligator, moving slowly towards me. I instantly stepped back, when, with a sweep of his tail, he brushed off several of my fish. It was certainly most providential that I looked up at that instant, as the monster would probably, in less than a minute, have seized and dragged me into the river. This incredible boldness of the animal disturbed me greatly, supposing there could now be no reasonable safety for me during the night, but by keeping continually on the watch. . . . It was by this time dusk, and the alligators had nearly ceased their roar, when I was again alarmed by a tumultuous noise that seemed to be in my harbour, and therefore engaged my immediate attention. Returning to my camp, I found it undisturbed, and then continued on to the extreme point of the promontory, where I saw a scene, new and surprising, which at first threw my senses into such a tumult, that it was some time before I could comprehend what was the matter. . . .

"How shall I express myself so as to convey an adequate idea of it to the reader, and at the same time avoid raising suspicions of my veracity? Should I say, that the river (in this place) from shore to shore, and perhaps near half a mile above and below me, appeared to be one solid bank of fish, of various kinds, pushing through this narrow pass of St. Juan's into the little lake, on their return down the river, and that the alligators were in such incredible numbers, and so close together from shore to shore, that it would have been easy to have walked across on their heads, had the animals been harmless? What expressions can sufficiently declare the shocking scene that for some minutes continued, whilst this mighty army of fish were forcing the pass? During this attempt, thousands, I may say hundreds of thousands, of them were caught and swallowed by the devouring alligators. I have seen an alligator take up out of the water several great fish at a time, and just squeeze them betwixt his jaws, while the tails of the great trout flapped about his eyes and lips, ere he had swallowed them. The horrid noise of their closing jaws, their plunging amidst the broken banks of fish, and rising with their prey some feet upright above the water, the floods of water and blood rushing out of their mouths, and the clouds of vapour issuing from their wide nostrils, were truly frightful. This scene continued at intervals during the night, as the fish came to the pass." The traveller is, for a change, frightened two pages later by two bears: a description I omit, though I cannot refrain from completing my extract with a further and final account of an alligator.

"... An old champion, who is perhaps absolute sovereign of a ... lagoon (when fifty less than himself are obliged to content themselves with swelling and roaring in little coves round about), darts forth from the reedy coverts all at once, on the surface of the waters, in a right line; at first seemingly as rapid as lightning, but gradually more slowly until he arrives at the centre of the lake, when he stops. He now swells himself by drawing in wind and water through his mouth, which causes a loud sonorous rattling in the throat for near a minute, but it is immediately forced out again through his mouth and nostrils, with a loud noise, brandishing his tail in the air, and the vapour ascending from his nostrils like smoke. At other times, when swollen to an extent ready to burst, his head and tail lifted up, he spins or twirls round on the surface of the water. He acts his part like an Indian chief when rehearsing his feats of war; and then retiring, the exhibition is continued by others who dare to step forth, and strive to excel each other, to gain the attention of the favourite female."

Wallace Stevens

THE IDEA OF ORDER AT KEY WEST

SHE SANG BEYOND the genius of the sea.
The water never formed to mind or voice,
Like a body wholly body, fluttering
Its empty sleeves; and yet its mimic motion
Made constant cry, caused constantly a cry,
That was not ours although we understood,
Inhuman, of the veritable ocean.

The sea was not a mask. No more was she.
The song and water were not medleyed sound
Even if what she sang was what she heard,

Wallace Stevens was an odd kind of insurance man—he wrote poetry on the side. His Collected Poems *won the 1954 Pulitzer Prize. "The Idea of Order at Key West" is considered the apex of his work.*

Since what she sang was uttered word by word.
It may be that in all her phrases stirred
The grinding water and the gasping wind;
But it was she and not the sea we heard.

For she was the maker of the song she sang.
The ever-hooded, tragic gestured sea
Was merely a place by which she walked to sing.
Whose spirit is this? we said, because we knew
It was the spirit that we sought and knew
That we should ask this often as she sang.

If it was only the dark voice of the sea
That rose, or even colored by many waves;
If it was only the outer voice of sky
And cloud, of the sunken coral water-walled,
However clear, it would have been deep air,
The heaving speech of air, a summer sound
Repeated in a summer without end
And sound alone. But it was more than that,
More even than her voice, and ours, among
The meaningless plungings of water and the wind,
Theatrical distances, bronze shadows heaped
On high horizons, mountainous atmospheres
Of sky and sea.

It was her voice that made
The sky acutest at its vanishing.
She measured to the hour its solitude.
She was the single artificer of the world
In which she sang. And when she sang, the sea
Whatever self it had, became the self
That was her song, for she was the maker. Then we,
As we beheld her striding there alone,
Knew that there never was a world for her
Except the one she sang and, singing, made.

Ramon Fernandez, tell me, if you know,
Why, when the singing ended and we turned
Toward the town, tell why the glassy lights,
The lights in the fishing boats at anchor there,
As the night descended, tilting in the air,
Mastered the night and portioned out the sea,
Fixing emblazoned zones and fiery poles,
Arranging, deepening, enchanting night.

Oh! Blessed rage for order, pale Ramon,
The maker's rage to order words of the sea,
Words of the fragrant portals, dimly-starred,
And of ourselves and of our origins,
In ghostlier demarcations, keener sounds.

Alison Lurie

K E Y   W E S T

THE SUN HAD come out again, and the sky was the color of a gas flame, but nothing she passed seemed real. The houses were too small and uniformly white, the sun too large and glaringly luminous, and everything that grew looked as stiff and unnatural as a Rousseau jungle: giant scaly palms like vegetable alligators; scarlet-flowering deciduous trees with enormous writhing roots and varnished leaves and long snaky pale brown creepers hanging down from above. Below them gardens burgeoned with unnatural flowers: oversized pink shrimps, glossy magenta trumpets with obscene red pistils, and foot-long crimson bottle-brushes.

The fauna were just as exotic and unreal as the flora. Huge

Alison Lurie divides her time between New York, London, and Key West. She teaches English at Cornell and is the author of several books, including Foreign Affairs, *for which she was awarded a Pulitzer Prize. This portrait of her Florida home is from the 1988 novel* The Truth About Lorin Jones.

speckled spiders swayed in six-foot webs between the branches of the tropical trees; little pale gray lizards skittered nervously along white-washed fences, then suddenly froze into bits of dried leaf. In one yard there were white long-necked birds the size of turkeys; in another a tortoise-shell cat as large as a terrier.

And then, even worse, there were the people. A bearded bum with a foot-long iguana draped around his neck like her grandmother's old fox fur; a woman walking two long-haired dachshunds in plaid boxer shorts; a man in a Karl Marx T-shirt and frayed canvas sandals getting out of a white Cadillac. A half-naked youth waved from an upstairs window; and in one of the flowering trees overhead a long-haired pirate in a red bandanna and gold earrings, pruning with a wicked-looking chainsaw, grinned and shouted at her to look out below.